O LORD
& the Queen

ALSO BY ELIZABETH STEVENS

NEW ADULT/ADULT BOOKS
Heaven & Hell Chronicles
Damned if I do
Damned if I don't
Damned if I know
All Devilbums Go To Heaven

Grace Grayson Security
Chaos & the Geek
Hawk & the Lady
O Lord & the Queen
Rollie & the Rocker
Tank & the Rebel

Loving the Sykes
Caden
Carter
Luther
Oscar
Ashton

MATURE YA/NEW ADULT BOOKS
the Trouble with Hate is…
Accidentally Perfect
Gray's Blade
Being Not Good
Popped

a GRACE GRAYSON novel

O LORD
& the Queen

ELIZABETH STEVENS

KINKY SIREN

Kinky Siren
An imprint of Sleeping Dragon Books

O Lord & the Queen
by Elizabeth Stevens

Print ISBN: 978-1925928808
Digital ISBN: 978-1925928792

Cover art by: Izzie Duffield

Copyright 2020 Elizabeth Stevens

Worldwide Electronic & Digital Rights
Worldwide English Language Print Rights

All rights reserved. No part of this book may be reproduced, scanned or distributed in any form, including digital and electronic or mechanical, including photocopying, recording, or by any information storage and retrieval system, without the prior written consent of the Publisher, except for brief quotes for use in reviews. This book is a work of fiction. Characters, names, places and incidents either are the product of the author's imagination or are used fictitiously, and any resemblance to any actual persons, living or dead, events, or locales is entirely coincidental.

This one's for all the fangirls, fanboys, fanbies, and fanpeeps. May your nerd light shine forever bright like a diamond.

♥

Contents

Raegan	1
Nico	11
Raegan	24
Nico	34
Raegan	50
Nico	62
Raegan	74
Nico	89
Raegan	108
Nico	122
Raegan	138
Nico	152
Raegan	163
Nico	181
Raegan	191
Nico	199
Raegan	208
Nico	217
Raegan	228
Nico	236
Raegan	244
Nico	251
Raegan	261
Nico	277
Thanks	288
My Books	289
About the Author	290

Author's Note

This book is written using Australian English. This will affect the spelling, grammar and syntax you may be used to. This might come across as typos, awkward sentences, poor grammar, or missed/wrong words. In the majority of cases (I won't claim it's infallible, despite all best efforts), this is intentional and just an Aussie way of speaking (it took my US beta readers a bit to get used to). I can't say 'the' Aussie way, since we seem to differ even within the same state. Just think of us as a weird mix of British and US vernacular and colloquialisms, but with our own randomness thrown in. I still hope you enjoy it, though!

A note on the whole Society aspect; I have to admit I've taken some liberties with this, but I've tried to combine them with a more realistic Adelaide lifestyle. This will hopefully not be too jarring, and explain if there are inconsistencies to the sort of Society you expected.

1
Raegan

The best thing about my workplace was that the carpark was underground and my desk was in the basement, which meant I only had to see as many people who happened to be as late as I was on any given day. I didn't have anything against people. I just had a problem with people who looked at me like I didn't belong.

Most of the suits at Olafson International looked at me like I didn't belong. It didn't help the dislike of the establishment I'd been cultivating since my early teens, and it had certainly cemented a dislike for people who wore suits like they were the only measure of successful adulthood.

Not that I was interested in what most people considered successful adulthood, but no one likes to be made to feel lesser than.

My boss, Duncan, didn't usually care if I was late in because he knew I'd both get the work done and I'd stay late as often as necessary. Most mornings, he just gave me a vague nod or wave from the desk in his office as I walked into the Dungeon, and that was about it. Which made his clear 'get in here' that Thursday morning oh so weird.

I dropped my satchel at my desk and wandered into his.

"Close the door," he said, not looking up.

"Uh…" I said slowly, closing the door behind me.

"It's bad, Rae," Duncan said, wincing in apology. "Really bad."

Oh, frak. This again. I'd hoped if I ignored it then it would go away. No such luck, obviously.

I sighed and my hands wrung for the umpteenth time that week. "Okay. But, like the Rohirrim are late bad, or the TARDIS blew up bad?"

He grimaced in a weird combination of humour and confusion. "Um… I'm not sure. Where does," he looked at the paper in front of him, "'Possible ties to criminal organisations, consider your employee in danger' fall on that scale?"

I felt the blood drain from my face.

"Sit, Raegan."

"Oh." I fell more than sat in the chair in front of my boss' desk. "That's more like Death Star is aimed at your house bad…" I looked up at him. "Does it really say I'm in danger?"

Duncan nodded. "I'm afraid so. Between potential retribution and media frenzy… They've suggested I get you some personal security."

I frowned. "Personal security like 'dark shades and an earpiece' personal security?"

"Yeah. Something like that. The firm Mr Olafson uses is generally pretty discrete."

I gave him a disbelieving look. "Discrete? You can pick those dudes out a mile away."

And I had. On numerous occasions. I couldn't remember a staff Christmas party where one of those suited goons hadn't been patrolling all serious and deadly looking. None of my 'Men in Black' jokes had ever gone down well with the big one in particular.

Duncan failed to hide his smirk. "Mr Olafson likes the…image of security."

"I'll say," I muttered. "And, I'm getting one whether

I like it or not. Aren't I?"

He nodded again. "Yep. 'Fraid so."

I sighed. "Well, can't we just chuck mine in some cargo shorts and a fandom shirt and say he's an intern?"

Duncan snorted. "I'll see what I can do. But you know what the big guy's like."

I nodded. I did know what the big guy was like. I'd worked for Olafson International for the three years, before I'd even finished university. Duncan was the uncle of my good friend Mel. So, when a position came up in the bowels of their IT Department and he knew I was perfect for it, he fought to get me the position.

Olafson International was by and large your basic multi-national and, I'll be honest, I didn't understand more than half the pies they had their fingers in. There were legal sectors and accounting sectors, real estate was bought and sold, information was traded, there were lavish parties, and my salary was good. So, I'd dealt with system maintenance, I'd done the 'have you tried turning if off and on again?' spiel about ten million times already, and I'd worked on updating their secure networking.

What I hadn't bet on was stumbling across a shady-looking money trail and a suggestion of human trafficking or something equally as glamorous. Which was why I was in the pickle I was now in. Because, I'd taken it to Duncan, who'd taken it to Mr Olafson, who'd taken it to the authorities, and somehow it had been leaked.

As far as we knew, we were the only three in the company who knew it was me who'd found it. But you'd think criminals would have some decent hackers, so I guessed the authorities figured it was only a matter of time before someone followed my e-footprints back to their source.

"Mr Olafson said the security company was organising their team to get you someone as soon as possible. Could be this afternoon, could be tomorrow."

"That soon?" came out as a squeak and I cleared my throat.

"Yeah. He was going to give me a heads' up to send you up to his office to meet them."

"You mean I'm going to have to leave the Dungeon?" I asked him, utterly aghast.

He nodded solemnly. "Sorry, Rae. But it's the only way."

"But no one leaves the Dungeon, Duncan... Not

unless it's *absolutely* necessary."

He shrugged. "I guess it's absolutely necessary."

I sighed and hung my head. "Fine. But, let the record state that I'm not pleased about this."

"You think anyone will be?"

A sudden thought hit me. "What are we going to tell Jackson?"

Jackson completed the Company of Nerds who ruled over the Dungeon.

Duncan frowned. "About what?"

"About why there's a security dude following me around?"

Duncan rubbed his hands over his eyes. "I dunno. We'll work it out. Oh hey, can we say your nan finally kicked it and left you the millions?"

I rolled my eyes. "He'll be all over that in a week."

"Shame. I'll sort it. Just be ready to meet the dude. Yeah?"

"Sure, because I didn't have anything better to do with my life."

Duncan huffed a laugh. "Go forth, Nerd Queen. Janice's email won't fix itself."

"Janice should stop giving her email address to sex

sites," I said as I stood up.

Duncan snorted. "Oh, but I don't possibly know how they got my email," he said in his sarcastic falsetto.

"The Wallbanger and Thrusting Swan winging their way to her front door say otherwise," I replied wryly.

"Not that you'd know anything about those things," Duncan said.

I pointed at him and tried not to smile. "I am far too pure, boss-man."

"No. 'Course. Miss Innocent of the Perpetual Single would rather watch *Touched by an Angel*."

I sniggered. "You shut up, Duncan. I don't see dates clamouring at your door."

Which was as surprising as it was unsurprising. Duncan was a lot younger than Mel's dad, which put him about ten years older than me. I think he'd recently had his thirty-fifth, maybe? I found it hard to keep track. But still, guy wasn't heinous, and he was falling behind in the nerd-knowledge compared to me and Jackson, so I didn't know why he didn't pull more tail.

He had that light brown hair and sweet brown eye combo and, had he not been Mel's uncle, then I might have even been inclined to roll the die on that one. But, between that and understanding adulthood required a modicum of professionalism, I'd put Duncan in the 'drool but don't touch' basket as soon as I became legal.

"Maybe not." He leant back in his chair and laced his hands behind his head. "But I'm not going to pretend I don't indulge in carnal pleasures."

I barely contained an epic snort. "I'm going to get to work before Jackson slaps a sexual harassment suit on us."

He unlaced his hands quick smart, but didn't lose the companionable smile. "Good plan. I'll let you know as soon as Mr Olafson calls."

I nodded, starkly reminded of the serious dive my life was about to take. "Cool."

I pulled his door open and saw Jackson's eyes snap up at the sound.

"Everything good?" he asked and I nodded as I threaded my way back to my desk through the piles of computer towers and parts and spare monitors that littered the Dungeon.

"Yeah. All good."

Jackson nodded and went back to focussing on his computer. I had to hand it to the nerd, he was even less adept at social interaction than me. At least I managed it with flair and an endearing bumble.

I dropped into my chair, picked up my pen, gave my David Tenant bobble-head a whack for good measure, and pulled up Janice's email account.

Managing to get lost all day in work, any hopes that I'd go home without having to meet whoever was sent for my bodily protection were dashed at four fifteen.

We'd long since stopped using our legs to covey messages in the Dungeon, so the notice came via an email that just said:

Mr Olafson's ready.

Why Janice hadn't just called me, I didn't know. But message received.

I nodded to Duncan to show him I'd got it, then pushed up from my chair.

Again, Jackson's eyes darted up. "Leaving early?"

"Nope," I replied, popping the 'p'.

"You don't need more coffee or the toilet yet."

"I sure don't." I mean, I could always do with more coffee.

"And you're not leaving yet?"

I shook my head. "Scotty's beaming me up."

His eyebrows drew together for a moment, then his

eyes widened. "Why?"

Jackson was the kind of guy to be laser-focussed. He took ignoring social mores to a whole new level. Normally, I applauded him his quirks. Just then, not so much.

"Who knows? Maybe Olafson's firing me?" I chuckled humourlessly.

"He shouldn't do that. You're the best here."

I nodded and pointed at him in agreement. "No. Thank you. If he tries it, I'll remind him of that."

Jackson gave me a nod as he went back to his computer screen. "Do."

"Good talk," I mumbled to myself and headed for the lift.

It felt wrong and weird to hit the up arrow but, like the adult I was, I did it.

As the doors closed in front of me, I felt a twinge of something unpleasant wash over me. It was like my whole life was about to change and I was not prepared for it.

"No one's trying to kill you," I reminded myself as I rode up the building. "This isn't a crime novel…"

2
Nico

I woke with a jump and heard a familiar voice talking at me. I was willing to bet the voice belonged to the foot that had kicked me awake.

"Coffee…" I rasped as I pulled my face off my desk and sat up, and opened my eyes.

A mug was waved past my face and I rubbed my hand over it in an attempt to wake up. All that served to do was further disrupt my glasses, so I had to right them before having any hope of seeing anything with my still-sleep-laden eyes.

"Remember that time you weren't going to sleep for a month?"

"What God forsaken time is it?" I asked, my voice no better than it had been before.

"Eleven. I don't have time for you to wake up. I need

you functioning now."

My chair went out from under me and I looked up into the no-nonsense face of Chaos.

"That was not excellent, dude," I said. "You want me functional, give me the good stuff."

"Get up and get to the War Room, then you get the coffee."

"No, no, no!" I whined as he walked out and I grunted in annoyance.

I dragged myself off the floor and pulled my half-awake, tired arse to the War Room after the much faster promise of coffee. Everyone was already there.

I picked up my tablet and followed the boss to the War Room, and found the others already there waiting for us. Hawk and Rollie were fighting over pastries, and Tank was pouring more coffee.

"Okay, let's settle down, shall we?" Chaos said, sounding like a weary school teacher coming up to the end of term.

"Aye, aye, boss man," Rollie said, spraying icing sugar on the table.

I took my seat and buried my head behind my tablet as per usual. Some days, I wasn't even doing anything exciting – I could just be refreshing emails – but they didn't need to know that. Let them think I was doing something on the dark web that protected some small corner of the world from harm.

"Here," Tank said, sliding a napkin over to me. "Saved you one."

It was the thought that counted in this scenario since I was the only one who liked the yellow iced doughnuts. Was it my fault if I'd taken a particular shine to that fake banana flavour as a kid and never grown out of it? At least it meant I always got two doughnuts to every one of their nasty strawberry and boring chocolate ones.

"What's so pressing you got the nerd up before noon?" Tank asked.

"Olafson needs us on a new job and he needs it yesterday," Hawk said, more perfunctory than usual.

"What's that got to do with him?" Rollie asked, kicking his head in my direction.

"I agreed to function in exchange for coffee. I don't see coffee," I mumbled pointedly.

Something wet and cold hit my face and I looked at Rollie. Slowly, my blinking turned to a frown.

"Do you want me to rig your place to blow?" I

growled. "Because I fucking will."

"Can we not antagonise Nico before he's alive on the outside as well, please?" a sweet voice said, and I looked up to see Bert walking in with a tray of coffee.

A part of me felt instantly better.

"Shouldn't you be at uni?" Hawk asked his little sister.

She smiled. "Yes, but I heard there was an emergency and Nico needed to be up. Ergo, helping."

"Thanks, love," Chaos said, looking at his girlfriend.

The only time the guy went to mush was when Bert walked into a room. Mind you, Hawk was the same and most of us weren't far behind. Chaos had got our arses through some fucking serious shit, and he only made it through because he was trying to keep Hawk alive to get back to his sister - while we all tried to keep *him* alive. So, we all had a lot owing to that little woman.

The fact she was the closest person who spoke my language was a bonus. She might not have been fully fluent, but she got me. She was the only one of the people who had the misfortune of calling me friend that I liked more than I didn't. I loved them all, but I was under no obligation to like them all the time. It was what made us more like family than friends.

When I'd first met Hawk's little sister in Chaos' apartment, I'd recognised a familiar soul in her and we'd clicked instantly. With Bert, I didn't have to be one Nico or the other. I could just be me. It had taken me off-guard to start with but, as time had gone on, I'd come to appreciate the relationship. Not that it had ever been in danger of being anything other than friendship. Bert may have been one in a million to me, but it had honestly never crossed my mind for us to be more until our mutual friend Petra had joked about it once.

After that, the whole Bert and me thing definitely had crossed my mind. It crossed my mind, then firmly vacated a split-second later. Which I'm pretty sure was why I could be myself with her – same way I was myself with the team: there was no pressure, no possibilities for failure, and no expectations. I was more than used to potential friends running in the opposite direction thanks to my stellar personality. I'd never been worried or afraid about that.

"Can we get on with it?" My voice still grated, and not just from the added annoyance my thoughts had caused me.

"Where's your suit?" Chaos asked.

"My what?" All I could think of was super-suits...

"We need you on a job, Nico. Plain and simple," Hawk said.

"Right, I'll get my computer." I made to get up, but Chaos stopped me.

"We need you on a normie job, Nico."

I blinked. "Okay. I must still be asleep. You want me to what?"

"Raegan Lane works for Olafson. She's found herself in some shit and needs detail."

"So? Can't one of you fuckers do it?" I asked, looking around the room.

They all shook their heads. "She needs it now and no one else is going to be free for round the clock detail."

Round the...? This was just getting better and better by the minute.

"I do have my own shit to do."

"Yeah, well your shit can be done from this chick's couch if need be," Hawk snapped and I wondered what had crawled up his arse and died that morning. I decided, for my health, not to ask him.

I snorted; the idea of me on a normie job was too funny. "Yeah, Olafson's going to want all my glory on a job."

"This is why you need the suit," Rollie said in wonder, the plan dawning on everyone in the room.

"Oh, hell no…" I breathed.

"Think of it as role play," Tank sniggered.

"I do not do any of you fuckers."

"It should be short-term." Chaos crossed his massive arms and I knew this wasn't a request from a friend, this was an order from my CO.

"Fucking…" I muttered. "Fine."

Chaos went into lecture mode. "Olafson flagged this with me a little while ago. Said there'd been some shady shit uncovered and to put us on stand-by–"

"Wait a second," I said, sitting up and pointing at him. He looked at me expectantly. "This is the thing, isn't it?"

"What thing?" he asked innocently.

It might have taken my sleepy brain a little too long to work it out, but I got there in the end. "The thing you… Ugh. This is the thing you were talking about before Hawk's engagement party."

Chaos shrugged. "Is it?"

Of course, it was. Olafson never did a single thing even vaguely related to security without running it by us first anymore. He wasn't Faulkner, but his nose still had a touch of brown on it.

"You said that was hypothetical. You said any change to my contract was only going to happen after a *long* conversation. You said not to worry about it."

He nodded. "And you don't have to worry about it. I've sorted out all the details, all you have to do is show up and get paid."

That was neither the point nor what I'd meant, and he knew it. I glowered at him, but Rollie got in before me.

"Wait on. Changes to contracts? If he's getting a pay rise, I think it only fair we discuss this as a group."

"No one's getting a pay rise," Hawk said quickly then looked at Chaos. "Are they?"

Chaos barely contained the eye-roll. "Nico will get paid accordingly, same as any of you on any job."

"But it's not a raise. As such?" Rollie checked.

"No," Chaos told him.

"Good." Well, that had Rollie happy.

What about me? "And when you say 'round the clock' and 'from her couch', that means literally around the clock and from her couch?" I looked between the bosses.

Which was somewhat of a farce. Chaos and Hawk

were in charge on paper, but we'd always – for the most part – made decisions together, as a team. But it didn't mean they couldn't delegate when necessary.

"There is a very real possibility her life is in literal danger," Chaos said gently. "That means I expect you to not leave her side until the danger has passed."

I frowned. "I've never done that sort of job before."

"No. But you're more than capable."

I was *almost* won over by the sentiment, but Rollie's words put a stop to that.

"Of being with another human twenty-four-seven?" Rollie laughed. "I would pay to see that."

"Rollie," Tank chastised in his quiet, deep voice.

Rollie had the decency to look somewhat chastened, but he still looked gleefully wicked and I knew he was waiting for the whole thing to bite me in the arse.

You and me both, brother.

Although I wasn't quite so happy about it.

"Get all your shit sorted as quickly as you can for working remotely, get some gear packed, change and get to Olafson as soon as possible. Contract starts today." Chaos finished like that was the end of it. No discussion.

We were in each other's shit books for now. But they

were the kind of shit books that would erase after nothing more a little bit of time. Family, and all that. So, I left it.

"Lucky I *don't* date. Expecting me to drop everything at a moment's…" I muttered as I walked out.

It wasn't a discussion. But I did get the last word in.

****

"Nicolas Daniels of Grace Grayson Security to see Mr Olafson," I said to Olafson's personal secretary.

There were perks to working for Grace Grayson Security. Namely, you got to walk most of the way straight into the boss' office.

She raked her gaze over my body and smiled welcomingly. "Just a moment."

She got up from her desk and exaggerated her hip sway as she walked to the big double doors on the other side of the room. I knew my eyes were supposed to follow her gait and they did so purely because there was nothing else to look at.

After a knock on the door, she popped her head in. "Mr Daniels from Grace Grayson, sir." A pause. A nod. A look to me. "He'll see you now."

I nodded to her and got past her with the least amount of body parts touching as I could manage. She was giving it her best shot though.

"Ah, good to see you," Mr Olafson said, standing up from behind his desk.

I inclined my head in reply.

"Ask Miss Lane to join us, will you?" he asked the secretary.

She nodded and was gone for less than a minute.

"She's on her way up, sir," she said, still eyeing me off.

"Thank you, Janice," Olafson said with a curt nod.

Janice had no choice but to leave.

We stood around in mostly awkward silence while we waited for Miss Lane.

"I hear Patrick's engagement party went well," Olafson tried for conversation.

Being me, I just nodded again.

When it came to security, I liked to rival even Tank's ability to be a stoic, silent wall. If only a slightly smaller scale. I'd rarely been allowed in the public – Mr Nelson's yearly gig was about it – but, when I was, I did my best to make sure no one had any cause to remember me.

Thankfully, it was enough to put Olafson off more small talk. The next noise, other than the ticking of a clock, was a commotion from behind the door. Next thing, a small body fell through it with an embarrassed giggle.

"You right, love?" I heard Janice say as the person tried to untangle themselves from a potted plant by the door.

"Yes. Yep. Fine. Thanks, Janice."

It was five words, but that voice did something to me.

Then the person turned around and I got a good look at her.

I felt my stomach plummet out of my arse.

She could barely have been five-foot-six, with dark purple hair, a thick fringe, and big blue eyes framed by black glasses. She bit her lip as she looked around the room and smiled sheepishly at Olafson. She wore wide leg jeans and her t-shirt had the freaking Millennium Falcon on it.

"Sorry, Mr Olafson," she said. "I came as quickly as I could."

"It's no problem, Raegan. I'd like to introduce you to…" Olafson looked at me, having already forgotten my name.

I hated dressing up. I hated role-play. But Olafson like things a certain way and damned if I wasn't going to do a job properly.

"Nico is fine, sir," I said in my best gruff imitation of one of my teammates, and Raegan's eyes snapped to me.

"This is Nico," Olafson said to the pixie dream in front of us.

She nodded at me. "Nico."

I gave her a curt nod in return. "Miss Lane."

I watched her mouth 'Miss Lane' like no one ever called her that and she had to remember it was her.

She had the makings of my own personal kryptonite.

"I do wish none of this was necessary, Raegan. But Grace Grayson have a stellar reputation. You'll be in good hands." Olafson turned to his desk to pick something up.

"If only," was said so quietly I couldn't be sure I'd actually heard her right.

"Sorry?" Olafson asked, turning back for a moment.

3
Raegan

I blinked.

Had I actually just said that out loud, or had I imagined it?

I cleared my throat and tried to think of anything remotely decent for public consumption. "Uh, I said I'm sure. I'm sure Nico will be very good at his job."

I mean, I *was* sure Nico would be good at his job.

I was also kind of keen to know what it felt like to be in his hands.

Because he was unnecessarily hot. Like unfairly hot. Like 'why do bad things happen to good people' hot. But then so was every single other Grace Grayson dude I'd ever seen. So why I'd expected this one to be any different I didn't know.

He wore a dark grey suit that looked like it had been

poured onto his body. His light hair was swept back impeccably and his blue eyes surveyed me with the practised ease of a man with too much confidence. He was chiselled and delicious, if a tad lankier than what I was used to with the Grace Grayson buffet. *Because buff...*

The dude was making me seriously reconsider my dislike of suits.

Well, no. He wasn't making me reconsider. All reconsidering had been done and my brain was wondering what it would take to get a guy like that into my bed. Based on the fact he'd barely looked at me, it would take a whole lot more than I was willing to give. Which was a shame really. But then, there was no way a guy like that and a girl like me had any future beyond maybe a couple of tumbles in the proverbial hay. Which made the effort seem even less worth the reward, brilliant though I expected it to be.

I pulled my mind (most of the way) out of the gutter in time to watch Mr Olafson give Nico an ID card and super sexy lanyard.

It would be sexy if it was the only thing he was wearing...

Bad brain.

"Raegan can have that set up to get you access to whatever you need. Kit said you'd know what to ask for."

Nico nodded at Mr Olafson, but didn't say anything.

Up until that point, I hadn't been aware that strong and silent was my type.

Mr Olafson continued, "I understand you know the parameters of the contract. Of what I'm paying for?"

Another nod from Nico. His silence didn't seem to faze Mr Olafson.

"Good. Good. Well, Raegan. I will leave you in the very capable hands of Nico. I trust you will keep me apprised of any developments on your end?"

One more nod from Nico.

Okay. The novelty was slightly starting to wear off now.

"Yes, sir," I answered, if only to spare Mr Olafson from having a conversation with himself.

Mr Olafson nodded. "Good. I expect Nico will need a word with Duncan, see the office and such before you leave for the day?"

It was clearly a question aimed at Nico, but he – *you guessed it* – just nodded again.

"I'll – uh – take him down to the Dungeon now then, sir," I said.

Nico's eyes flew to me at the word 'Dungeon' and I almost regretted my word choices. Almost. I didn't know what he was thinking – whether that was a good, interested look or a bad, shocked look on his face – but I wasn't okay with being embarrassed for being me so I told myself to get over it.

"Thank you, Raegan. Let me know if you need anything." It was a dismissal and I was happy to comply, even if the last words hadn't been directed at me.

"Thanks, sir. Will do." I looked at Nico. "To the Dungeon, then."

Nico inclined his head in a way that wasn't *quite* a nod, but also totally was because he was agreeing with me. I'd never noticed how much one nod could convey before. Like, people actually *could* communicate wordlessly.

"Okay, then," I said, as much to fill the silence and to stop myself thinking about how sexy wordless communication looked on this particular suit.

As we walked to the lift, I wasn't quite sure who was leading who. Nico somehow managed to lead but also be following me since, naturally, the guy didn't know where we were going.

The ride down in the lift was awkward to say the least. It was the kind of awkward silence that defined awkward silences. So, of course, I filled it with rambling conversation.

"So, Duncan's our boss. He's great. Real supportive and totally professional. Really lucky to have him. Then there's Jackson. His last name's Pollock, but I call him Pillock. Not to his face, obviously. That'd just be rude. Jackson's a family name. Pollock was his parents' name. Best not to mention it. They hate art. Especially modern art. But especially body paint.

"He's fine. Just intense. And super pessimistic. Like, very doomsday. Likes reminding you of all the bad shit." I looked at the silent, suited deliciousness, not that he was giving anything back. "Not you. Obviously. He hasn't met you. But the royal you. General you, if you will." I saluted, as you always have to do to generals.

"Whatever, right? So that's the Dungeon. It's a mess," I laughed, sub-consciously willing myself to shut up. "But it's our mess. You know?"

I looked at him again.

He was just watching me with slow blinking eyes like he couldn't believe he'd been given me. Like he couldn't believe he was so unlucky as to be stuck keeping my mouthy arse alive.

I cleared my throat. "So, they really think my life's in actual danger, huh?"

"Yes," was all he'd say on the matter before he turned his head to see how much longer he'd have to be stuck in a lift with me.

"Helpful," I muttered to myself. "So…Nico, huh?"

He nodded.

I sighed. "Good talk, man."

I half expected, with my luck, that the lift would choose that moment to break down and we'd be trapped until the next morning. Thankfully, it reached the basement safely and the doors opened.

I stepped out hurriedly, tripping on the pristine, flat carpet. Nico's hand shot out towards me as though he was on autopilot.

"Uh," I chuckled as I rearranged my glasses. "Thanks."

Another nod.

"That's gonna get real old," I said quietly.

Nico's arm moved to the doors but I waved him away.

"This princess saves herself," I told him. I chose to believe he didn't get the joke rather than think I wasn't witty, so I clarified, "I get my own doors."

His eyebrows rose slightly as though in question. "And if the room were occupied by hostile forces?"

I swallowed all the stupid answers. "Okay. Fine. I don't get my own doors."

I waited while he pushed the doors open to the Dungeon. He looked around quickly then indicated I precede him in. As I did, I immediately looked to Duncan's office. He must have been waiting for us because he was looking our way.

I did the best 'point and eye roll' at Nico I could manage while I was walking in front of him. Duncan smiled.

"I need a word with your boss," Nico's deep voice said.

"I need…" I put a stop to that quick smart!

Because the last thing I needed to do was tell him I needed him to go back to just nodding so my brain wouldn't disappear to fantasy land every time I heard his voice.

It was good.

Too good.

It was discovering there were such things as porgs good.

It was the love between Geralt and Jaskier good.

"I need to go and see if Janice has bought any more vibrators," was a *way* better thing to say than what I'd stopped myself from saying.

For a split second, I thought he looked intrigued. But I knew I'd been mistaken when he – yep – just nodded and headed for Duncan's office.

Duncan rose to meet him as Nico closed the office door. I watched the two men shake hands and get into what looked like some pretty serious talk.

I did my best Nico impression and nodded to Jackson before scurrying to my desk.

As I tried to pull my eyes off Duncan's office and go back to my work, I felt a sense of dread settle over me.

Duncan's face was serious.

There was seriously a security guard being paid to keep me safe. To protect my actual life, if all accounts were to be believed.

It was suddenly all kinds of real, and I was starting to

feel a little bit concerned about the whole thing. I pretended I didn't as I went back to my day job and got lost in that for a little while.

But, eventually, I snuck another look up from my computer and saw Nico and Duncan were still sequestered away in his office. Nico was standing over Duncan's shoulder and watching whatever Duncan did on his computer monitor. Every now and then, his eyes would flick up at me.

It felt less like he knew I kept watching him and was retaliating, and more simply the practised art of his profession. Did he actually expect that I was going anywhere? Let alone that I'd be capable of doing such a thing in the five second interval between glances?

Quite aside from the fact that I wasn't about to leave anyone down in the Dungeon at the mercy of Duncan and Jackson if it wasn't necessary, there was also my health to consider. Or lack of health, as it were. As in death.

As Angella Dravid said: unhealth is dead.

Now, I wasn't going to say that I totally believed my life was actually in danger, or that I was going to be targeted by human-trafficking mobsters. That sort of thing only happened in books and movies. Or maybe overseas. It certainly didn't happen to insignificant IT techs in little old Adelaide, Australia's murder capital and city of serial killers though we might be.

Some people might not think my life amounted to much, but I was quite attached to my current level of health so I was going to let the buff-but-lean, sexy security dude in the suit look after my person. It'd frankly be rude not to.

"Rage!" Jackson hissed and I thanked his timely intervention.

My brain had been about to dive down a dangerous rabbit hole

I looked at him. "Yeah?"

"Who's the guy in the suit?"

I chewed my pen as I tried to think of something. Nothing remotely plausible came to mind. "Uh…some security thing Mr Olafson organised." I shrugged.

Jackson frowned. "And why did you have to go and meet him?"

This was why I called him Pillock in the privacy of my brain. I was all for everyone living their quirkiest life, but the dude could be super annoying.

4
Nico

My eyes were already irritating me, and I'd only been wearing my contacts for a few hours.

It just added to the general irritation about my person.

Listening to Duncan prattle on about their security system had been one thing. Understanding it intimately when he first showed it to me, but still having to listen to him 'explain' it all had been another. But I was a good role-player. Not that I'd go to the extent to allow myself to be called a LARPer, despite how live action this whole thing was.

Also adding to the general irritation about my person was the call to Chaos as I followed Raegan and her little yellow Beetle 2.0 back to her house. It had to be a yellow Beetle, didn't it? It couldn't have been something more covert, less conspicuous. Couldn't have been a white

Toyota. It had to be a Beetle. It had to be yellow.

I'd said nothing when I first saw it and I was putting that in the too hard basket for now.

"What's she like?" I heard Rollie's voice.

Because, of course, Chaos had decided to make it a conference call.

"None of your business," I replied.

"Come on, she's some tech nerd." That was Hawk. "Think female Nico."

I stretched my neck. "She's nothing like me," I answered stiltedly.

"Ooohhh!" Hawk and Rollie teased.

"Sounds like someone's got a crush on the target!" Rollie sang. Shame he put such a good voice to such poor use.

"Please. Unlike the rest of you, I'm plenty capable of keeping it in my pants."

"No one said anything about sleeping with her," Hawk said slowly and knowingly, and I inwardly cursed.

"You were all thinking it." Correct, but also obviously covering up my previous tell-tale words.

"Sounds like we weren't the only ones," Rollie chuckled.

I rolled my eyes as Raegan turned a corner and I followed suit, thankful the team couldn't see my face and give me even more shit. "Whether I'm thinking it or not is irrelevant. I've got a job to do and I'm doing it."

"Doing *her* more like," Rollie stage-whispered.

I chose to ignore him. If I didn't, there was a potential figurative danger I'd think too long about doing her and forget there was an actual physical danger to her life, which was far more important than whether I got laid or not in the foreseeable future. There was, at least, one benefit to the call then.

"I've gone over the building's security. Physical and electronical. The physical isn't brilliant, but the electronic is passable. Have we got any details as to what I'm meant to be looking out for? Can I expect to be jumped by the mob? Foreign intelligence? Just some other security detail?"

"On that front, Olafson has very little," Chaos said and I could hear shushing noises in the background, followed by a distinct thump and an 'ow'. Chaos continued like nothing had happened, "I assumed you'd be able to find out more." It wasn't a question.

"The IT head went over the full system with me.

Finding the back door in shouldn't be a problem. If I can find some trace of–"

Rollie – I knew it was Rollie – gave an exaggerated yawn. "You'll nerd out and find the wankers, got it."

"Remind me why these arseholes had to be involved," I said dryly.

"Because we're a team," Rollie said, sounding half-injured and half-peppy.

"Because," Chaos corrected him, "the more of us abreast of this the better. We're mostly paid so our clients look even richer. If there's a life on the line, we're pulling out all the stops."

I stretched my neck as I watched Raegan pull into a driveway and I slowed to a stop at the curb in front of the house. "I get that, I'm just not sure what having them sit in on phone calls is accomplishing."

"It accomplishes a lack of inter-office memos," Hawk said.

Hawk had an aversion to inter-office memos. Mainly because he had a habit of losing them. It wasn't my fault if he sucked at filing and organisation.

"We could be thirty-seven percent more efficient if we used them," I told him for the thirteenth time.

"We would not because I'd spend thirty-seven times as long trying to find anything."

"Maybe that whole personal secretary thing isn't such a bad idea?" Rollie's voice suggested far more than his words.

"The last thing we need is for Flo to be interviewing new secretaries for you every week because you lacked professionalism," I snapped.

"Putting aside memos and secretaries for the moment," came Tank's voice, always the voice of reason. "Is there anything we can be doing to help you at the moment, Nico?"

I sighed, watching Raegan get out of her car.

Even getting out of her car, she had this…energy to her. She practically bounced. On any other woman, it was the first 'wrong way, go back' sign I'd been known to ignore. When it's only one night, a little extra energy is never a bad thing.

"Just…reach out to your contacts and see if there's anything circulating. Surely there's some mutterings about this somewhere, which should give us more idea of what to expect."

"Can do," Tank answered.

"Let us know if there's anything else," Chaos said. "If you get a moment, the next Ultiron thing is ready to go when you are."

"And when am I getting this moment while I'm on round the clock detail?" I asked, looking pointedly but uselessly at the screen in my dash.

"If you're suggesting we should look into hiring another resident nerd–"

"It's fine!" I huffed. "I'll do it overnight."

Raegan was hovering next to her car with her satchel and shielding her eyes against the sun as she looked at my SUV.

"I've gotta go and check out what kind of shitstorm I'm walking into now," I muttered. "O Lord out."

Old habits die hard.

I hung up on them with my call sign, deciding I didn't need to wait for them to say goodbye. We might have used mostly different tech these days, but comms were still comms and I was technically in the field.

I pulled myself together, picked up my gear, and got out of the car. I pushed aside all thoughts about what she looked like, what the expression in her eyes might say, or what the neighbours would think if I just threw her against that horrific Beetle.

"Good. You made it," Raegan chuckled nervously. "I was starting to think you'd just camp out in your car all night. You know, covert stake out or something."

Not knowing what the hell to say, I just waited for her to lead me to the front door. I wasn't so devoid of social mores that I was going to go to the door first.

Raegan started up on her rambling again. "It's Wheaton Road. Did you see?" she said as she started rummaging in her bag as she walked. "It's kinda big for just me, but I took the place just so I could make the joke when people asked my address." I looked at her blankly. "You know, it's like… 'Wheaton!'" was cried the way Sheldon yells it then, at no input from me, her smile dropped and she cleared her throat. "Never mind. Good talk."

I felt bad. My nerd senses were tingling and I was actually kind of impressed with her. But I wasn't being the guy who appreciated a *Big Bang Theory* joke. I was being the guy who didn't know what that was.

"Do you need to open this door as well or am I allowed to unlock my own home?" she asked, holding out a bunch of keys.

My eyes scanned quickly and efficiently as she jiggled the keys in her hand.

Based on the case notes, it was unlikely any of her personal information had leaked. But it never hurt to be overly cautious. In my world, it meant more than a loss of income.

I kicked my head towards the door, indicating she could do it herself.

"Gee, thanks," she muttered as she unlocked her door.

I could tell she was the sort of girl to make this a lose-lose situation. Whether I gave her a continuous rundown of all the pertinent information or said nothing, whether I opened every door or none of them, it'd be wrong.

It irked me.

As she opened the door, I rearranged my shoulders in my suit. It was tailored to my body shape perfectly, but it was still uncomfortable. Restrictive and uncomfortable. Add that to my eyes feeling itchy and dry, and the fact I was shackled to this woman for the foreseeable future all made for one extra prickly Nico.

Raegan led me in. Her nervous waffle was drowned out as I took everything in. And not just because the place was a nerd's perfect home.

I could do my job and appreciate her sense of interior decorating.

The house was typical for just out of the Adelaide CBD. A little double-fronted cottage, all stone and English garden. The interior was to be expected as well. The layout. The décor should have been expected but still pleasantly surprised me.

Part of me felt like I'd walked into the ultimate comic store. There were books everywhere and Pop Vinyls everywhere else. Where the walls weren't covered in bookshelves, there were fandom prints. The Marauder's Map. Marvel *and* DC characters. The Death Star. A collage of Doctors. The door under the mountain. And that was just what I could see from the front door. Even my eyes couldn't scan quickly enough to pick up all of them.

She noticed me looking as I was staring at a Twilight poster. Can't say it was my thing, but it gave me all the information I needed to know that's what it was.

"Uh," Raegan chuckled self-consciously. "Heh, that's uh… Guilty pleasure from my teens. Nostalgia and all that, you know." Another chuckle.

She looked down as she closed and locked the door

again. I stood to the side of the hall. My gear was heavy. Tank had spent hours training all of us, but I was still more lanky than muscular, and dead weight was dead weight.

"So…" One more self-conscious chuckle. "This is my place."

I spared her a nod out of sheer politeness.

"Okay. Uh, well, I don't know if you have stuff to set up. Do you have stuff to set up?"

I nodded.

She gave me a less sure nod in return. "Then feel free to set up wherever suits. I've got a study. There's the kitchen table. I only use that for parties. I guess that's off the table if someone might be trying to kill me."

There was hope in her voice, so I gave her another nod to dispel any fantasies about what this was. We had no real evidence – just advice from the authorities – that her life was in direct danger, but the team from Grace Grayson took a certain pride in our work for the money we were paid. The only good thing about this job was the extra money I'd see for it.

"Right. Thought as much." She nodded and started leading the way down the hall. "Um, so yeah. Help yourself…to whatever. There's tea and coffee – just the instant kind, I'm afraid – bread for toast, spreads and that are in the fridge or pantry."

The hall opened up into the open plan back; kitchen, living, dining. The windows were large. What I could see of the yard looked secure, but I'd have to check to be sure.

As I was taking everything in from a solely security-minded angle, she was hovering.

"Is…everything okay?" she asked.

I nodded, finally bringing my eyes back to her.

"So, what have you got to set up? Cameras? Perimeter sensors? Heat detectors?"

I felt my eyebrow rise of its own accord.

"No. Sure. Someone's been watching too many spy movies." She looked around the house. "But honestly, what kind of intrusion are we talking here?"

Had no one briefed her on the mission parameters?

"You drive me everywhere, I wonder what you get up to night and day without me, then we pop back into each other's lives for a couple hours? Something like that?"

I took a deep breath and aimed to sound as polite as possible. "I'm on round the clock duty," I explained.

She looked at me. Her eyes narrowed as her mouth twitched like she wanted to ask me what I meant, but wanted more to figure it out for herself. I was an impatient man.

"I'm not leaving your side until the threat is passed."

She blinked. "Oh. Uh. Right." Her hands waved between us. "Not like…same bed…or?" She paused to look at my face then nodded. "No. Not that. Okay."

I didn't know if she was pleased or disappointed. I didn't know if I was pleased or disappointed. I thought it best not to try working it out.

"Uh. So, where are you sleeping?"

"Couch is fine," I told her.

She frowned. "I have a perfectly acceptable spare room."

"I don't sleep much."

Lies. I loved sleep. I slept as much as possible.

But, aside from the fact I was playing a role here, I also didn't want to get too comfortable. Comfortable made for less alert.

She nodded again. "Okay, cool. What do we do now then?"

"Just go about your business. You can pretend I'm not

here."

She spluttered a laugh. "Yeah, no," she said as she sobered and I saw her eyes run over my whole body. "I can… I'll just… Yeah, I'll do that." She looked around. "So, I will do that then. Do you eat? I planned chicken for dinner but…?"

I didn't know the protocol here. Not first hand. There were jobs you agreed to dinner, there were jobs you didn't. I just didn't know what kind of job this was yet. I didn't know if accepting dinner stemmed more from other ideas I entertained of her, or if it was the innocence of needing to eat while working. I could always pretend it was the latter.

"Chicken is…good." I gave her a nod. "Thanks."

"Okay. Then I'll go change." She gave a small smile and started heading for the hallway.

"Where do you spend most of your time?" I asked quickly, totally not thinking about the fact she was about to get at least partially naked.

She blew a strand of hair out of her face. "Couch, mostly. Unless I'm in bed." A look crossed her face that suggested she was thinking nothing pure. "Sleeping, that is. I didn't…"

"Sure. I'll take a closer look around."

"You do that."

And I did. I started outside. It was the furthest possible I could get to her while she was changing.

As far as jobs went, it was standard. The fences were high enough that a grown man would have trouble jumping it without help. Problem was, help abounded. There were gardens and trees sprawling all over the backyards in this suburb. Big, old trees. The garden just in this yard alone was busy enough someone could hide here without being easily seen, particularly at night.

Cameras might not be the stupidest idea after all.

I finished my survey of the outside, judging it passable, though not ideal. I could work with it, especially while the threat was high but not as immediate as some other jobs. I'd look at setting cameras quickly.

When I got inside, she was in the kitchen prepping food. I did my best to ignore her singing to herself as I looked over the interior. Mostly windows and doors. Potential weak spots. I logged them all away. Inside matched outside; I'd worked with less.

While I waited for her to finish dinner, I sat at the dining table and made up some schematics of the place, changes and tech that would help me keep Miss Lane safe. As usual, I got so wrapped up in my work, my eyes only darting around out of pure training, that I only half-registered her put two bowls on the table. It wasn't a threat, ergo I ignored it.

"Dinner is served. We at chez Raegan appreciate you spending your time with us, and hope everything is to your satisfaction." She sat across from me. "No. Wait. That was a bit more airline than restaurant." She shrugged and pushed one bowl towards me.

It smelled good, and I realised I hadn't eaten since the night before. Typical, but I ate like a human.

As we ate, she talked. "So, does Mr Olafson usually hire security for the insignificant staff members?"

I spared her a glance, but said nothing.

"I just didn't know if I'm special? Or if this is just par for the course for him?"

I still didn't say anything.

She grinned. It lit up her eyes. "Unless that's an 'I'd tell you but then I'd have to kill you sort of thing'?"

It wasn't. I knew why Olafson had done it. The man hated debts. If Raegan got killed, that would have been an epic debt. It was also the right thing to do. Olafson had flaws, but he was decent.

"I'm going to need a little something more if we're both coming out of this sane," she said, waving her fork at me.

"Consider it employee benefits," I told her.

She nodded. "Okay. That's something."

She prattled about this and that, trying to draw me into conversation. It was easier than I expected to play my role. I had no idea how to talk to someone like her. She reminded me of Bert with her exuberance, but where Bert had these moments of reserve Raegan just jumped into something else, always moving, always talking. Sometimes, she sounded nervous but others it was like that level of chatter was just normal for her. Much like with Rollie, every moment of silence had to be filled.

By the time she decided to go to bed, I was rethinking what her voice did to me. I was exhausted.

"Okay... So, night then," she said with an awkward wave and a bob of her head.

I nodded, glad it was early enough I could get the Ultiron thing done and still get some sleep.

5
Raegan

It wasn't Nico's total hotness that turned me into a bumbling idiot in his presence, it was the silence. It was the fact he refused to say more than the bare minimum, and that made me antsy.

Quiet people and I had never got along. Reserved people and I had never got along. To be fair, a lot of people and I had never got along. I understood – and loved – that I was an acquired taste. And I did even worse when the other person gave me nothing. I could do positive reinforcement. I could do negative reinforcement. I enjoyed riling people up as much as getting along with them. But no reinforcement? It left me feeling adrift. I had no idea what to do with that. No idea what parts of me to emphasise or downplay. The result was a nervous, giggly wreck.

So not attractive.

Normally, I'd tell myself it didn't matter. Who cared if the rando security dude thought I was attractive enough! Right?

Wrong.

Not this time.

This time, I was keenly aware of what I must look like to this gorgeous man who wasn't supposed to leave my side until my life was safe again. I got it was unprofessional to try to sleep with your security guard while he was on the job, but a tiny and farcical part of me hoped that maybe I'd have a chance after. Like when he was no longer on the job. If I could actually maintain some sense of…well, sense around him until then.

The first night had not been a brilliant example of how wonderful I was.

So, I resolved on Friday morning – after the best night's sleep I'd had in years – to show him exactly how awesome I could be.

To say it could have gone better might be an understatement of epic proportions.

I was showered and dressed and feeling surprisingly human by seven thirty, which was impressive considering I hadn't voluntarily woken up before eight since that one Christmas when I was seven and my aunt took me to the beach until it was a somewhat more civilised hour.

When I got to the kitchen, Nico was changed and had a mug to his lips.

I tried very hard not to think about where he got changed, how he got changed, and by how much I'd missed seeing him getting changed. For about five seconds. I then told myself to grow up because he was totally not standing there thinking about me naked.

"Morning," I said, almost disgusting myself with how sweet I sounded.

This well-rested Raegan was a strange creature and I wasn't sure I liked her.

"Hey," Nico replied.

Well, that one word did two things. Firstly, it told me that he had definitely had some amount of sleep. Secondly, it gave me a worrying concern my knees might be about to buckle. For a woman who thought twice – three times – about waking up next to a guy in the morning, I could stand to hear Nico's morning voice as often as possible.

"Sleep well?" I asked.

"Fine."

I told myself we must have made progress because one word was definitely better than nodding. I was rethinking that when it came time for him to tell me to get into his car to go to work. He sounded pissed. The angry kind. I felt my chest constrict a little at the idea I'd offended him or something, but was mollified some when we got to the office and he just rasped, "Getting more coffee," at me.

Smiling to myself, I tried not to start a tally of things that Nico and I had in common.

Firstly, because Nico showed no signs of interest in me – why would he, he was a suit. Secondly, because he was undoubtedly way more professional than I was. And thirdly, because I wasn't attracted to suits.

"Say it with me now," I muttered as I dropped into my chair.

"What?" Jackson asked.

I shook my head. "Nothing, man. All good."

He gave me a thumbs up and went back to work.

****

Friday night was no better than Thursday night.

He drove me home from work. I made dinner again. I attempted vague conversation with him while we ate and wondered why we didn't just eat on the couch. At least then I could have flicked through the telly, and the awkward silence I kept filling might have seemed less awkward.

Luckily for me, my very best of friends weren't taking no for an answer when I told them I was staying in and demanded I video call them.

"Well?" I asked, showing them my entire person.

"All right," Filmore said. "I will officially accept that you're not dying or about to adopt a million cats."

"No," I laughed. "I'm just staying in on a Friday night. It's not unheard of."

"True," Mel agreed. "But you know the rules."

I did know the rules. Rules stated that anyone who pulled out of something last minute must be checked for breakdown-syndrome, deathbed-ed-ness, and hermit-itis. Which sounded worse than it was; it was just our way of taking care of each other.

"I do, and I've fulfilled them. Now, may I go and have a Friday night to myself? I'm trying to adult up in here."

The fact I also had Nico in my house and was hoping to hide that from them at all costs had me wanting to cut the call short. It would take far more explaining than I had the brain power for at that time.

Mel rolled her eyes and I knew she wanted to thump me. "Where did this sudden obsession with following the norm come from?"

I put on my best wise voice. "Insanity is doing the same thing over again and expecting a different result."

Mel snorted. "I have no interest in the 'sane' you, and you don't either."

I sighed tiredly. "True." I shook my head. "True."

"How was work?" Filmore asked.

I shrugged. "Same old. Same old. You guys?"

"Yeah. Same. Same same, but different."

"God. Our lives are riveting."

We looked at each other and laughed.

"Do you remember when we actually had the energy to go out five nights a week?" Mel asked.

"I remember it, but I don't believe it happened. Why would we do that to ourselves?"

"We could stop, you know."

"I'm missing one night, not suggesting we stop altogether," I told them.

"That's what you say," Filmore said.

I rolled my eyes. "And what else would we do for our mandatory weekly get together? High tea on a Sunday? Please don't say a bike ride around Adelaide's finest trails then coffee at Cibo in our lycra." I fake-gagged.

Mel smiled warmly. "Do you even know where Adelaide's finest trails are?"

I shrugged. "The Torrens?"

Filmore grin suggested that was unlikely. "What do I look like? A cyclist? Health aficionado? I don't know. Mel?"

"I don't…*cycle*," she said like it was the most absurd idea ever.

"You don't cycle…yet," Filmore said.

Mel was constantly on new weird and whacky health kicks, trying to get us to join her in an effort to 'preserve our bodies'.

"I suppose we could stay *in* and drink…" I said slowly, trying out the idea in my mouth.

"Are you ready to admit to we're getting older?"

"My body is. My mind is. My pride, not so much."

"Sounds about right."

"What are we looking at tonight, then, O queen of the nerdlings?" Mel asked and I knew what she meant.

"Yeah," Filmore added. "We don't all have live-in boyfriends we can jump at our disposal."

As far as relationships went, I'd never been lucky. Guys of any age just didn't seem to want the nerd. Not long-term anyway. And pardon a girl for not wanting to change in order to attract a mate. Mel called me stubborn to spite my face. I called me realistic.

What was supposed to happen? I doll myself up for the night, talk about things I know nothing about, and act all demure and sweet to get the guy to want to date me. Then what? A few months later, when I'm smitten and he's realised I'm a foul-mouthed uber nerd, I get my heart broken. No thanks. Easier to be single and swipe right on Tinder when the need arose.

But there wasn't much chance of that. I could just imagine asking Nico if it was okay if I popped out for a bit to meet a Tinder match. I'd have much preferred to stay in and just ogle him anyway. I just couldn't make use of him nor mention him to my friends. Thus, my excuse.

"I dunno." I sighed. "I'm not really feeling it."

"You're not feeling it?"

Oh, I was feeling it. There was a guy in my living room I was all up for feeling. He had me very ready for *feeling*.

"There's just no remotely interesting guys out there," I said.

"I'll try not to take offence to that, shall I?" Filmore asked with a shit-eating grin.

I smirked at him companionably. "You know what I mean."

His only answer to that was a nod. "Aside from yours truly, is it just me or does every guy out there look the same?"

Which was true. Filmore's hair was currently green and blue, bright and vibrant. Thursday night was his salon-at-home night so his hair would look pristine for whatever shenanigans the weekend brought. We didn't seem many like him around.

"They do," I concurred. "They all look like corporate wankers."

"Probably all investment bankers with EY."

"Do EY have investment bankers?" Mel asked.

"No idea." He shrugged.

I knew how he felt. Like me, he worked in IT. We'd met at uni during our computer science undergrads. I could sort systems and fix computers, but I had no idea what my big boss' company were involved in most of the time, and Fil was the same. Most of that was on me. I treated my job like it was need to know. There was enough work that I didn't need to go looking for what would potentially become more work.

Except in the cases I did.

"You two are going to have to get out of your comfort zones if you don't want to keep going home alone," Mel pointed out, and I wasn't thinking about a certain suit.

"Excuse me for not abandoning my morals just for some horizontal refreshment."

"You need to stop sending him material." I looked at Mel accusingly.

She shrugged. "Sorry, not sorry. It's funny."

Mel was a history buff. She loved all things old-timey. Books. Styles. Phrases. It came from a deep-seated belief in tradition, and she was a firm believer that there were some things that absolutely *must* be brought back into circulation. Like Victorian slang for sex such as 'horizontal refreshment'. It was her favourite era.

"It is funny, Rae," Fil agreed.

I held my hands up, careful not to drop my phone. "Okay. I know when I'm outvoted. Horizontal refreshment stands."

In their defence, it was funny. In most cases, it was an apt description of the act. I also just enjoyed knowing that the Victorians (era, not state) were actually not as stuck up and stuffy as we'd been led to believe. If I'd been interested in history, outside the rise of science-fiction as a genre, I think I would have liked the Victorian era too.

"Now, go forth and find Fil some of this horizontal refreshment. There's a Spiderman marathon with my name on it waiting for me." I waved my hand at them in a shooing motion.

"Fine." Mel held her hand up and sighed. "Fine. Fil, we'll see you in a couple minutes?"

He nodded. "Yep. Meet you there."

"Say hi to Jake for me," I said, meaning Mel's boyfriend.

"Will do."

"Bye!" we all chorused and closed the chat.

I lay back on my bed and sighed.

After the week I'd had, I hadn't felt like going out at all. I'd seen no sense in worrying my friends by telling them the real reason why. But I still didn't like not telling them things.

I went to bed way too early again, not even taking into account the fact that I didn't have anywhere to be the next morning. Or day. I spent a good hour reading and telling myself not to make an excuse to go out to my living room again. That would have been embarrassing to say the least.

'Oh, Nico. I'd hoped to see you here. I just wanted you to see me in my PJs because isn't the baggy t-shirt and shorts look so super sexy?'

Yeah, hard pass.

He made me a little delusional, but not so delusional as to think that would work.

6
Nico

Chaos had scheduled a video conference for Saturday morning. Morning. Saturday. Two of my favourite times to be asleep.

Raegan wasn't awake yet and I was more than happy to have a moment to myself. As it were. Even though it was being interloped by four total wankers.

One night stands were simple. You went in, did the deed, and got out. No names. No numbers. Minimal talk. No personalities. It was the very definition of quick and easy.

Friends, on the other hand, were not simple. Family was an obligation it was difficult not to love anyway. Despite best efforts. The Grace Grayson team straddled the line between friends and family far too much for my liking.

And all I wanted was to sit in front of my computer, away from the inanity of it all.

Chaos and this mission had taken that away from me, and then some, so my team would have to deal with the guy waiting for them to join the call for once in his life; sleeping had proven elusive in an unfamiliar situation and place.

"Mornin', Nico," the boss' voice came over my speakers.

I grunted, finishing off a note on my tablet at my elbow.

"Avengers assemble and all that."

I looked up and actually allowed myself a smile. "You're making a one-way trip to the dark side, man."

He shrugged like it wasn't a big deal that he'd fallen in love with his best mate's little sister and it had turned his whole world upside down for the better. "I hear you bastards have cookies," Chaos said.

I huffed as I took a sip of the God-awful excuse for coffee Raegan had in her house. "Anything we haven't already eaten is way beyond the realm of safe human consumption."

He nodded once. "Yeah. I don't doubt that."

"Bert eating you out of house and home?"

"Doing her best."

"PhD confirmation's soon though, yeah?"

He nodded. "Not soon enough. I think everyone just wants it over."

"She worried?"

"She'll be fine. Her supervisor thinks the world of her."

"I didn't ask if *you* were worried."

He smirked at me knowingly. "I'm aware even the best laid plans fall apart. She knows what she's doing, but I want her to do well."

"Don't we all, man."

Tank's face popped up yawning.

"At least someone's doing worse than me," I muttered.

"You working again tonight?" Chaos asked Tank.

He nodded and stifled another yawn. "Late shift again."

Chaos gave a single nod and looked at his paper. "Don't forget to note your hours. Rough estimate will do. Rollie, looks like you've got a lunch with Jefferson's wife?"

My eyes flicked up and saw Rollie and Hawk had arrived. Everyone was at home. Everyone but me and Chaos. Rollie grinned around a doughnut and opened his mouth, but Chaos cut him off.

"I don't want to know the details."

"Plausible deniability and all that," Rollie agreed with a wink.

Chaos muttered and shook his head before continuing. "Thanks for doing this on a Saturday. I know it's unusual, but we're working with unusual at the moment. Hawk, you're going in to meet the new clients at three, but otherwise off all day?"

Our technical office hours were nine to five, Monday through Friday, but one or more of us was constantly going in to do something or was rostered on for some job. We were lucky our receptionist, Flo, was as accommodating as she was to come in on a weekend when we needed her. There were very few days we all had free at the same time anymore.

"Yep. I have to leave on time, though–"

"Naw, your old lady expecting you home for dinner," Rollie teased, but we all knew it was actually good-natured.

Hawk gave him a nod. "Yes, actually. I promised her we'd finally choose a colour scheme tonight since she's got a brunch this morning. Priscilla's getting antsy about sending out the save the dates."

"I thought you hadn't picked a date yet?" Tank said.

Hawk shrugged. "Apparently you don't need a date to start ordering the *papier* and *bomboniere*."

"I think the word you're looking for is *bonbonniere*," Rollie said.

Hawk shook his head. "That is not what the paper shop calls it."

I looked up at the sound of his voice and saw his face matched it; he looked like he'd made that mistake and been told off so many times and so strongly that he wasn't about to do so ever again.

"Well then, the paper shop is wrong." Not that Hawk's face stopped Rollie arguing it.

While Hawk and Rollie were debating that, another voice popped through from Chaos' mic. "Chaos, Falkner's on the line for you."

"It's Saturday. Can you tell him I'll call him back?"

"Already tried that."

Chaos sighed. "Okay. Thanks, Flo."

"Sure thing, boss."

"You lot behave. I'll be back in ten," Chaos said to us, then we heard him muttering, "Fucking Falkner," before he left the meeting.

As soon as he was gone, Hawk and Rollie turned into the class gossips making the best use of the time while the teacher was out of the room.

"Two down. Who's next?" Hawk asked, looking around.

No one had to ask him what he was talking about.

"Nico?" Rollie suggested with his cheeky grin.

I was not thinking about small IT professionals with purple hair and glasses. "Fuck off."

"Naw." Rollie clasped his hands under his chin and batted his eyes at me. "With poetry like that, they'll be flocking to his door."

"Leave the nerd be," Tank said gently.

"The gentle giant speaketh!" Rollie pointed at him accusingly through his camera. "Will it be you? Already got someone in mind? Eh?"

Tank shook his head with a hint of a smile at his lips. "You seem very keen to point the finger. Are *you* hiding someone?"

Rollie snorted. "Pfft. Like I could hide it if I was getting some on the regular."

They all nodded in agreement, and I had to admit I was kind of glad Rollie relied on client's wives, daughters and friends to get his jollies. Had he been dating anyone, it would have been worse than Hawk and Chaos combined with the gushing and the smiling and the unprovoked laughing. I wasn't so naïve as to think the three of us still single lads were going to stay that way forever. At least, not the other two. Well, one of them. Tank was a catch and no mistake. But I wasn't exactly looking forward to any of it.

"If you had to pick someone, who would it be?" Hawk pressed. "Who's next?"

"Seriously, Nico," Rollie suggested and Tank looked thoughtful.

I scoffed. "Yeah. I don't think so. I'll be the confirmed bachelor, thanks."

"What's so wrong with a long-term commitment?" Hawk asked and I looked at him over the top of my glasses.

The action was purely aesthetic; I couldn't see jack shit without them. "Have you met the team from Grace

Grayson?" I answered. "We sleep with the clients so we don't accidentally get hitched." I pointed at him in sarcastic shock. "Whoops."

Hawk grinned from ear to ear. It was almost contagious. "Yeah. That happened."

Deep down, I was glad he was so ridiculously happy and in love. The slightly shallower part of my personality didn't really care for it.

Rollie sniggered. "All this 'twue wuv' running around is making a guy wonder if it's such bullshit after all."

I rolled my eyes behind my computer.

A year ago this hadn't been a problem. A year ago no one was engaged or co-habiting or trying to get us to talk about our feelings over very important conference calls. A year ago we were just a bunch of guys getting by day to day as best we knew how. Which, let's be honest, wasn't all that well at all.

Now Chaos was loved up and shacked up. Hawk was loved up, shacked up, and planning a wedding. Rollie was throwing around words like 'date' and 'romance'. Thankfully Tank kept his mouth mostly shut on the subject – same as he did with any subject, actually – and nothing suggested he was hiding any secret mistresses.

Yet.

And I was left behind, perfectly happy where I was, but uncomfortable they were all moving on without me. I already had very little in common with the average human being. Being assigned after basic training to those arseholes had been as much a blessing as a curse. What was going to happen to our tight-knit group when they all settled down and that was one less thing I had in common with them?

Because I was never settling down, shacking up, or finding a happy medium.

It was difficult enough to find a girl who spoke my language – figuratively, obviously. Even if I did manage the insurmountable task, I couldn't be the guy who could picked *that* up and manage to actually pick that up. It was what Chaos the CEO called a growth area; I was either full nerd and turned into a condescending robot, unable to talk to anyone like a proper human being, or I was what Rollie referred to as the one-night-stand-king. And that guy wasn't exactly conducive to a lasting relationship.

I had no plans to work on any of my growth areas, let alone that one.

To date I'd had no reason nor inclination to try mixing

those personalities, but the task would have been impossible anyway. Mostly because – and I could admit it – I was an arrogant shit unwilling to lower myself to the inanity of the general populace. Most people mistook my disdain of the mundane for shyness, and I saw no reason to correct them. No need to draw out the interaction.

Besides, while I wasn't going to dumb myself down for people to understand me or actively try to engage with me, I also did actually do my best to not be an outright dick.

Still, that was another of my growth areas.

"…Nico'll be the last of us to settle down," Chaos, back again, was saying as I tuned back in to the general hubbub.

"Thank you." I nodded.

But Chaos continued, "Women like flattery and the ability to hold a conversation."

This new Chaos was a pain in the butt. "Sexist much?"

He nodded. "True. Thank you. *Everyone* likes flattery and the ability to hold a conversation."

I scowled at him. "And here I thought I still had hope with half the population," I said sarcastically.

Chaos flashed me a grin. "Shit outta luck on that one, mate."

"Oh, damn. Whatever shall I do?" I asked, deadpan. "Die alone and unbothered. Oh, wait. That was my plan anyway. Lucky me." I gave them a split-second smile. "Can we get back to work now?"

"You wouldn't be in such a hurry if I walked in here and said Amber and I got engaged," he said as though that was some big reveal.

I shrugged as I went back to my tablet. "*That* would be interesting. Nay. Relevant."

"I distinctly remember you making Chaos talk about Bert moving in," Rollie pointed out. "Should he not be able to make you talk about girls?" It sounded like the question had more to do with his uncertainty in the correctness of his sentence.

"No," I said simply.

"Whelp," Rollie said, and I heard the resigned shrug in his voice. "You heard the man."

"Fine," Chaos said. "Tell me what you've got on this Olafson International business."

We tried not to let the darker aspects of our jobs stop us from living life. In other words, we hid all the dark shit behind humour. We functioned as members of society – to varying degrees of success – because of our coping mechanisms. Be they jokes or a short segue into irrelevant twaddle.

But, when it came down to it, we were professionals.

7
Raegan

Eventually I fell asleep, and woke up on Saturday morning to a Nico who was looking a tad more dishevelled than the previous day.

He was standing in my kitchen with a mug in his hands again. Only that morning he was also looking every bit the morning after dream. His clothes were rumpled. His tie was off, his top button undone. His sleeves were undone and rolled haphazardly up his arms. His hair was messy like he'd run his hands through it absently a few too many times. And he was still rubbing his eye.

"Well, good morning," I practically purred and decided I wasn't actually awake enough to be using my mouth. Clearly the mouth-brain connection hadn't quite kicked in yet.

He looked at me, his eyes sliding down and back up my body slowly. For the briefest moment when our eyes met again, I thought I saw some answering smoulder in his eyes, some instinctive reaction to my tone of voice. A thrill ran through me and I stopped myself from playing with my manky first-thing hair in what passed as flirting in my book.

He looked away as he swallowed another sip and nodded. "Morning."

"You really don't sleep much, do you?"

He shrugged. "Not a job spec."

I smirked. "Was that a joke?"

He looked at me and his expression was completely deadpan. He didn't need words. His eyes said it all; 'What do you think?'

"If you told me, you'd have to kill me?" I teased.

Nico lifted the mug to his lips again and I imagined he was hiding a smile. "Sure."

I set to making my own coffee and I noticed he didn't leave the kitchen as quickly as he had the previous morning.

"That stuff is shit," he told me.

I turned a sarcastic grimace on him. "Then why are

you drinking it?"

"Caffeine."

"Ah, a man after my own heart."

No! No comparisons! You are not similar. He is not interested. More to the point, you're not actually interested. Leave it alone.

I nodded, hoping we could skim over that whole sentence.

"I suppose going out for a coffee would be against the rules?" I hedged.

"Not the best idea."

I sighed as I went to put the milk away and realised the fridge was empty. "On a scale of good security to bad, is going to the supermarket or having them deliver better or worse?" I asked.

He didn't say anything, so I turned to look at him. His expression was thoughtful, like he was actually considering the question. So, I just waited for his answer.

"Get it delivered."

"Ten bucks says you just don't want to be seen at the supermarket with me. C'mon, Coles is right around the corner. If we don't, I might have to feed you tuna mornay for dinner."

It was my go-to pantry meal. So long as I had milk. I loved it. I was also aware that plenty of people didn't.

He shrugged. "You don't have to."

I nodded. "Yah-huh. I don't have to if we go shopping. They also have a café…"

For a second, I thought I'd won. Nico actually looked at his coffee mug as though whatever was in it had betrayed him and anything else would be better. But then he looked to me and shook his head once.

"Ah, but you were tempted!" I told him.

Again, there was a moment where I felt like I'd invited, or was being invited by more with my words. He looked me up and down, quickly this time like he hoped I wouldn't notice.

I noticed.

I just didn't know what to do about it. Did I lay the flirting on heavy and see where the morning took us, or did I try and retain some modicum of dignity and decency by not throwing myself on him and begging him to ravish me now? The latter seemed like a better, more adult option.

"Okay," I said, louder than necessary. "Ordering it is. We can always get pizza tonight?"

Nico nodded.

"Uh, have you… Have you got everything you need?" I asked him.

He gave me a blank look.

"Clothes. If you need to wash, feel free. Um…shower is—"

"Shower would be good."

I was trying not to think about him in the shower. I failed. "Oh. Uh. Good. So, bathroom is…well, you know obviously. You've not *not* been to the toilet for…" I cleared my throat. "Good talk. Yep. So, I'll get you a towel. And then I will order some groceries."

I did what I said, plonking myself at my computer just as I heard the water start running. In an effort to not picture a wet, naked Nico in the shower, I forced myself to focus on groceries.

To some degree, it was a good thing I quite often over catered for one person so I'd had, to date, enough to feed the both of us. I'd still not quite mastered the art of living alone. It was so expensive to cater for one. Much easier to cater for a million and freeze the leftovers for lunches. So, I tried not to buy more than I usually would, because that would easily feed Nico as well.

At least, I hoped it was okay that I was just assuming to feed him. It seemed the least I could do if he was sleeping on my couch to keep me safe. Yes, I knew he was being paid for it, but that didn't solve the immediate problem of him eating. And I *was* cooking for a small army anyway.

After Nico was showered and changed and groceries were ordered, I spent the day cleaning. Weird for me. It wasn't born out of an inability to reside in the same room as him without imagining him just ravishing me then and there. It was more the fact I sensed he didn't really want to be in the same room as me if he could help it. Friday at work, he'd been in and out, on computers and in Duncan's office, talking to his team and Mr Olafson. Other than that, he'd had one eye on me at pretty much all times. But we hadn't really been stuck together.

Not like Saturday.

I was hyper aware of him in my house. Not necessarily in a bad way, but in an 'I really want to offer to alleviate his boredom without it sounding way too sexual and probably failing' kind of way. Because the guy just seemed to spend his day cycling between perimeter checks, checking his email, getting shitty coffee, and standing around doing nothing. Job or not, I felt bad for the guy. Like who in their right mind would choose that as an occupation?

Then again, I guessed there'd be quite a few people who wondered who in their right mind would choose IT services as an occupation. So, there was that.

Still, I kept my mouth shut and kept my hands busy until it was time to deal with dinner.

"What do you feel like? Tuna or pizza?" I asked him.

He shrugged. "Whatever."

So, that was helpful.

"Okay. Pizza it is. How do you feel about pineapple? I'm told this is a point of contention among people, though I've never experienced it."

He looked at me. "Whatever," he said again.

"Super. Okay, I'll get the usual and you can suffer the consequences if in fact there are consequences to suffer."

"Okay."

Ugh. Fine. I didn't need him to be helpful. I reminded myself he wasn't a roommate and he wasn't a friend, and he certainly wasn't a potential lover. I was getting me pizza for dinner and he'd just have to eat whatever I was having because he was there.

It wasn't until I was getting ready for bed later that I realised that was probably his point. His being super unhelpful was actually him being accommodating. At least, that's what I chose to believe.

After going to bed so early for the two nights previously, by Saturday night I was wide awake. I'd read for an hour. I'd tried getting myself off – purely in the pursuit of relaxing, of course – only to freak out that he could hear me or knew what I was doing, and then given up entirely. I'd tried my mindful breathing, which to date had proven itself a crock of crap for me. And I'd tried not trying to sleep.

Instead of lying there in the dark and staring at the ceiling, I decided to just get up.

I found him at the dining table in the half dark, staring at his computer.

By the eery light of the screen, he looked exhausted.

His suit jacket and tie were off and he was just in his shirt and pants. His sleeves were rolled up again, his top buttons undone. He looked the epitome of the guy who's just come home from work and realised someone frakked up and he has to fix it remotely before he can go to bed.

But there was something else about him.

I studied him and wondered what my half-asleep brain was trying to tell me.

It was trying to tell me that Nico looked different. A difference that made me realise something about him the rest of the time; it was probably the first time I'd seen him when he hadn't been what could only be described as switched on. Every other moment I'd been with him – which had been *a lot* in the last two and a half days – he'd had a certain vibe about him. A vibe that was obviously 'on'. Which made sense really given that, in the most extreme circumstances, any lack of attention from him could mean someone died.

I tried not to think about the fact that the someone in this circumstance could have meant me.

"How many emails does a security guard have to check?" I asked him teasingly.

He looked up quickly, but didn't say anything.

Then I noticed his laptop.

"That's not the latest quad core–"

"Couldn't tell you," he said quickly and something felt off.

"You don't know what kind of computer you have?" I asked.

He shrugged, his eyes darting back to the screen.

I nodded. "Of course, you don't." I chuckled lamely. "Why would you?"

Why would he? He wouldn't. He wasn't the nerd in the dungeon who lived for computer tech. He was a highly trained security guard who probably did all sorts of shady shit in a former life to even pass basic qualifications.

He was still looking at me like he expected me to say more. I couldn't very well disappoint.

"How many hours of sleep do you run on anyway?"

"Varies."

"On the job?"

"Sure."

"Okay. So, on a job like this?"

He was watching me, but he looked down and scrubbed a hand over his eyes. "As little as possible."

"Okay, but is that like I stayed up to catch my US teammates online late, or I accidentally read until sunrise late?"

He looked me over like he had no idea what the scale represented. "Four hours. Maybe."

I gave an impressed whistle. "Phew. Okay. And I

thought I ran well on little sleep."

Not that, just then, Nico looked like he was running well on such little sleep. I guessed that was one reason he mainlined coffee harder than I did.

I realised he wasn't going to say anything else, so I asked, "Can I get you more coffee, or…?"

He wiped a hand over his eyes and sat back with a nod. "Thanks."

I didn't understand it, but I'd been made aware that there were some people for which using computers was difficult beyond simply browsing the internet or word processing. I didn't completely want to make assumptions about what Nico was doing, but it looked like it was proving difficult.

"Anything…uh…" I started. "Anything I can help with?"

"What?"

I kicked my head towards his computer. "Anything I can help with? I am somewhat proficient with *comp-u-ters*." I pronounced it like Jen on *IT Crowd* out of habit, but doubted he'd realise that. Too late now.

He shook his head, stretching his arms up onto his head. "No. Thanks. We're just running out of leads. I don't think it's so much that they've hidden their tracks well as that they haven't left any tracks to follow," he said like he was almost talking to himself. He frowned and shifted to do something on the laptop. Then frowned again. "Nothing," he sighed.

"So, what's the consensus? I am or am not in danger?"

Nico shrugged as I handed him his coffee. "Fragments say yes. Who from? I can't figure it out." He rubbed the bridge of his nose and his eyes. "It's like they stumbled across your stumble and haven't got the skills to do any more." It sounded like he was thinking out loud. He shook his head again, as though he disagreed with himself. "I don't even know anymore."

I wasn't going to shut his theory down. It was the most I'd heard him talk, and I liked listening to his voice. There was something oddly non-suit-y about it which made me think he still wasn't switched back 'on'. Whoever this Nico was, he was the closest to the real deal I was going to come. It was a shame, because I wanted to know more.

As though he could read my mind, he looked up sharply and I watched his eyes change. They didn't go cold, per se. But they sharpened. They lost that sense of soft, natural ease. This was the 'on' Nico.

"Mr Olafson said it was probably better that I leave it alone," I said, partly hoping to draw him back to that 'off' Nico and partly not knowing what else to say.

He nodded. "Sensible. The less connected to you, the better."

"You seem tired. Are you sure you don't want to make use of the spare room?"

Looking at me wearily, he almost smiled appreciatively. "I'm fine. Thanks."

I shrugged. "It's there if you want. I know for a fact that it's better than the couch, even if it's only a few hours."

There was a larger hint of a smile in his eyes now. "I'll keep it in mind."

I felt like that was the best I was going to get out of him and, short of getting unnecessarily pushy or weirdly flirty, I figured it best to leave it there.

"I meanwhile have had too much sleep the last couple of nights, hence my return from the bedroom," I told him, partly by way of explanation as to why I was up again when I said I was going to bed and partly just to continue the conversation.

He nodded, but said nothing. Just sipped his coffee.

"I don't usually go to bed so early," I huffed a laugh. "Especially on the weekend. Like what was that?" I laughed again, trying to ease the awkwardness I thought could have just been me.

"Just pretend I'm not here. Go about your normal routine," he said. His voice was mono-tone and I was only seventy percent sure it stemmed from him being genuinely polite.

I nodded. "Okay. I will...actually do that. In that case, mind if I put the telly on?"

For a second, Nico looked at me like he had some choice words to say but was holding his tongue. Eventually, he just nodded and got up from the table.

As I settled in for some traditional Saturday night re-watch of *Doctor Who*, he did another perimeter check. When he finished, he sat on the comfy lounge chair. I wasn't sure if he thought he was being sociable or was actually interested in the show.

After a few more episodes and a few more perimeter checks, I heard a noise from the comfy chair and looked over to see Nico asleep and snoring softly. It was more breathing really. He must have really needed the sleep to pass out like that, so I turned down the telly, and left him while I watched a few more episodes until I was finally exhausted enough that my eyes were threatening to close.

    I left Nico where he was and headed for bed.

8
Nico

Four days. Four days and I knew the kind of person she was. I knew she was a person my person could be interested in.

Raegan wasn't an enigma.

She was totally transparent.

Not that that was a bad thing.

She wore her personality on her sleeve and she wore it proudly. She could be taken at face value, and that value was high in my book.

She was the nerd queen of my dreams. Stupid smart. Sassy. Quick. Clever. Lover of all things cult, sci-fi and fantasy. The fact she was damned easy on the eyes – and unnecessarily enticing to rather lower down – was an added bonus.

The downside?

Putting aside the fact my perfect woman was essentially a client, the only downside was that she seemed to dig the stiff and proper jarhead type. And that wasn't just an excuse made up by the side of me who pretended he wasn't afraid to let other people see him for himself. That was substantiated with evidence – as Bert would say.

What evidence?

Numerous times, I'd been sure she was flirting with me. Her voice had bounced between turning me on and making me want to rip my ears off so often it was giving me whiplash.

"This," I muttered to myself as I scanned once more for anything on Olafson International's servers. "This is why I'm not allowed in public."

While my not being allowed in public was a serious issue, there was one more pressing. I'd found plenty in the servers. Plenty I was sure even the IT department hadn't seen. But nothing obviously related to Raegan's level of safety.

I sat back in the dining chair and blinked rapidly. My eyes weren't used to wearing contacts at all, let alone something like twenty-hours a day. I'd given them a bit of respite when I'd showered that morning, but it hadn't been quite enough. I had been tempted to take them out and just pretend to watch the movie with Raegan the night before, but watching movies wasn't why I was wearing them in the first place.

"You okay?" Raegan asked and I turned towards her.

She was in her usual comfortable combo. Today it was cargo pants and sneakers, and a hoody with a 'Good Omens' reference on it. I was in, surprise surprise, another suit.

I nodded. "Fine."

As she went about getting breakfast, she looked at me like she didn't believe me. "You sure? Because your eye is watering."

She wasn't wrong. I wiped it.

"I know my beauty is wonderous, but there's no need for actual tears. I am truly human, just like you," she said.

She wasn't facing me, but I could hear the smile in her voice.

It was things like that that attracted me to her. Her immediate appearance went some way to doing that as well. But over the last four days, things like that made me more interested in her, made me want to know more. She was clearly taking the piss to a degree when she said that kind of thing. But I knew she was also serious. Her self-confidence was off the charts. And I found that sexy.

She was a nerd. She was cute. She was funny. She was sexy.

I was in trouble.

On Thursday, I'd tried focussing on the job. I'd planned to ignore my instant, visceral reaction to her because I had a job to do. I'd mostly succeeded except for a few interloping thoughts about her getting changed.

Four days later and even my stubbornness had lost out.

Pity my role-playing wasn't the only reason I had nothing suitable to say to her. Even if I ditched the strong, silent persona she was quite clearly into, I'd be just as talkative.

Like now. I had no response to her words. I thought she was amazing for saying it, but had I replied I was sure the first thing out of my mouth would have been something more like, 'I wouldn't call it beauty making me cry', or 'It's my contact'. I couldn't even think of anything witty to flirt back with as an option of what I should have thought of.

That was how well I was geared for human

interaction.

"And crickets…." she laughed, turning back to me with her mug clasped in her hands. "Good to know you're just sitting there constantly daydreaming about how beautiful I am."

I blinked and she nodded.

"I'm joking. Obviously."

If only she knew she actually wasn't.

She leant back against the counter and looked me over as she took a sip. Her eyes were entrancing. They seemed to be a combination of come-hither and this easy teasing humour I knew from Rollie's eyes. Somehow, I didn't want to punch it out of hers. I wouldn't have been averse to kissing it out, though.

Oh, bad Nico…

Fuck, but I was definitely in trouble.

Like every other woman I'd met like her – like me – if she had any interest in mating with her own kind, then it was vastly overshadowed by my sorry excuse for the buff, butch, alpha jarhead type. Not that I didn't put every effort into it, but I was nothing compared to the rest of my team. It put a slight dampener on the whole 'my person could like her' thing. It was kinda difficult to like someone you knew wouldn't like you. Assuming I could be the sort of person she could actually like, which was a whole different problem altogether.

She just smiled at me, finished her breakfast, and we headed into Olafson International. Thankfully, she hadn't argued or questioned me driving her and the whole issue about her yellow Beetle had been avoided for a while longer.

"Huh," she said as she checked her phone in the lift up to her office. "That's weird. Duncan's never called me before work before. But he and Jackson have called like six times each in the last half hour."

The lift dinged to signal we'd reached our floor and she looked up from her phone as though the answer to her unasked question would be standing in front of her.

As soon as we stepped out of the lift, I could see why she'd have a bunch of missed calls from the office.

To the untrained eye – namely every employee on any floor above us, it looked much the same as it always did. I'd seen the place twice and even I knew better.

Through the glass doors and walls, it looked like a hurricane had torn through the Dungeon. Not that I'd heard of an actual hurricane ripping through Adelaide.

Unless you counted the ones from Hobart over Summer. Which was about the extent of my knowledge about sport. Thank you.

Parts were broken. Papers were strewn.

Someone had been looking for something.

I looked at Raegan.

Or someone.

"Oh my God…" Raegan breathed as she hurried forward.

I stuck my arm out to stop her. No way was she running headfirst in there on a good day, let alone when I didn't have a clear line of sight to most of the room.

My brain was running too fast.

I was on auto-pilot.

Nearly ten years of on-and-off training kicked in.

I grabbed Raegan, pulling her close to me as I spun to put my body between hers and the IT office. My eyes scanned quickly for somewhere to put her while I checked the office. There were few options. None were without risk. The least of them was the cleaner's cupboard though, so I wrenched the door open and threw her in.

"Stay here until I come for you," I ordered.

I waited only long enough for her to nod, then shut the door and approached the office.

It was a poor design in many ways. Any intruder would easily know we were there. They would have seen me shove Raegan in a closet and they'd see me now coming towards them. I was less worried because I was still between them and her. Also less worrying was the fact there was a chance I'd see them as well. If they were worth their salt, then they'd be hidden in a top vantage point. I had to hope their salt was worth very little.

I walked into the room slowly, my eyes constantly scanning for any sign of movement. There was nothing. Now I was in the room, I could see it was even more wrecked than my initial assessment. There were pieces of parts strewn around the room like some uber nerd with zero cares about the environment had decided it would make good confetti for their wedding.

I picked up some debris off Raegan's desk to try to work out what the intruders had been looking for. Was it related to Raegan's safety? Did they know who she was? Did they know how to find her? Thinking it would be a hell of a coincidence if it wasn't related, and that whoever it was had clearly targeted the IT department, I had to assume yes.

But all signs pointed to they were well gone by now.

Keeping an eye on things, I went to the cupboard and knocked on it.

"It's me," I told her.

She opened the door, her face whiter than usual.

"What's the damage? Is anyone dead?"

"Basic break and enter. They turned the place over," I answered as we went into the office.

She looked around in panic. "Duncan? Jackson?"

I looked around a little more calculatingly. I wasn't expecting to find a couple of dead bodies spread-eagled around the room after my initial sweep, but I was going to be prepared to find them.

"Is your address on file?" I asked her.

She stopped looking for her colleagues and looked at me. "Uh, why?" Her eyes went wide. "Oh my God, Mrs Warner…" she breathed, her hands darting to cover her mouth.

I frowned. "Who's Mrs Warner?"

"I used to rent her granny flat. The address on file… I never got around to changing it. It's still her place." Her eyes snapped to me. "Do you think they'll kill her?"

I had no idea who *they* were, so how I was to know what *they* would do was beyond me. Worst case protocol it was.

I pulled out my phone and dialled Chaos. He answered on the fourth ring.

"You're up early," he teased.

"Breach," I told him.

We had few code words really. At least very few official ones. But words like 'breach' gave us a quick and efficient way to reroute a conversation from joking to serious without wasting time.

"Report," he answered and I heard him typing in the background.

"IT offices at Olafson International. Obvious break and enter. Intruders looking for something. Possibly someone. Assume breach occurred over the weekend. Worst case, they're going to Miss Lane's previous address. The home of a Mrs Warner." I looked to Raegan.

She gave me the address and I relayed it to Chaos.

"On it," he said. "Coordinate with Olafson. Find out what he knows and what he's done. Authorities will need to be informed. Olafson will be all over the insurance claim. My end will deal with Mrs Warner. What's your plan for Miss Lane now?"

"Full home lockdown's our only option–"

"What?" Raegan spluttered and I looked up to find her gawking at me in disbelief. "Us? On lockdown? Together? Where?"

"She raises a good point," Chaos said. "If her address isn't on file, you could be safe there. Nothing I've heard suggests we have real hackers in play."

If Raegan was half the hacker Jackson seemed to think she was, she'd have covered her e-footprints and hidden her real-world identity as much as possible. I had. I defied even Jackson's opinion of her to trace my e-prints back to my real-world address through my various proxies, random generators and firewalls.

"What are our other options?" I asked, purely intel-gathering.

"We really haven't got the infrastructure set up for this sort of thing." I heard Chaos sigh. "Short-sighted on my part. But since when does this happen in Adelaide?"

A quip about us being the murder capital of Australia came to mind. I didn't think it would be helpful to raise that now.

"Her house it is. Timeframe?"

"Plan for a week. I'll get the guys out tomorrow to supplement your survey."

He was the one who'd forced me on this mission. "You're questioning–?"

"I'm not questioning your competence," Chaos assured me as I heard the lift ding again.

I stepped in front of Raegan and faced it.

"What time?" I asked Chaos, relaxing slightly as I saw Duncan and Jackson in the lift.

"Let us know what suits and what you need. I'll get the boys to pick whatever up."

I nodded. "Will do. I'll report in later."

"Understood."

"O L…" I was not saying that in front of people. "Nico out."

I hung up on him and looked to Duncan, ignoring the inquisitiveness on Raegan's face. But before I could say anything, Jackson spoke.

"Morning', Rage," he said as he looked around the mess.

I couldn't help pausing to look between them questioningly.

Raegan might have had a big personality, but I

couldn't picture her angry. Not rage-out angry. Not like Hu–

"It's not like, 'me Hulk' rage. Obviously," she chuckled awkwardly and I could have melted on the spot. "Look at me."

Oh, I was looking at her. It was bloody lucky I was being paid to look at her, because I could hardly stop looking at her.

"Like Raegan. Raeg. Rage," she continued with a shrug. "It's my tag. My screen name."

"All hail the queen of nerds," Duncan said with a soft smile as he surveyed the room, and Jackson nodded.

Raegan's smile was even more self-conscious. "Pfft. No." She shrugged again, slightly more wildly. "Well, I mean it was either this or try breaking into the FBI and hoping they gave me a job or something."

God help me. This girl wasn't just smart. Her brain didn't just go to all the same nerdy places mine went. She was perfection. Pure, utter perfection in a brilliant package. She deserved nothing short of perfection. And the only persona I had that could even come close would have pushed her away faster than Rollie climbing out the window when the husband came home.

"What's more important," Raegan said and pulled my stupid head out of my arse for me, "is what happened here?"

I internally forced myself to focus. If she was asking the pertinent questions while I was mooning over her, someone was bound to get killed.

"No idea," Duncan said. "Were we in one of those police procedurals you enjoy so much, I'd say we were broken into by some sort of criminal enterprise."

Here, Duncan shot a look at me. Had I been your average protection detail hired nerd, I'd have given the whole game away. As it was, I managed to hide my reaction from Jackson, as Duncan and I had agreed to keep in him the dark as much as possible.

"Why would a criminal enterprise be breaking into the Olafson International Dungeon?" Jackson asked.

Honestly, if they knew half the shady shit Olafson had dipped his toes into in the interests of making money – or by just generally being a weak-willed, easily led idiot masquerading as a shrewd businessman – the idea wouldn't seem so far-fetched.

"We've just been up and spoken to Mr Olafson. I've got access to the security feeds. We'll hopefully know more soon."

Soon wasn't enough to ensure some people's survival.

"We have to move all operations off-site," I said.

"All operations?" Duncan asked.

I nodded and checked Jackson was out of earshot. "If they traced Raegan's footprints back here, then it's only a matter of time before they trace them back to her specifically. All three of you are going to have to go into lockdown until this blows over."

"Lockdown?"

"We have to effectively shut down the department."

"Shut down?"

I was running out of ways to say it. I was out of patience. "Are you stupider than your position suggests, or just in shock?"

That did it. He frowned. "Fingers crossed for shock," he said sardonically and Raegan snorted. "Is it actually that serious?"

I shot a look to Raegan, who was watching me carefully. I was pretty sure I'd given away far too many facets of my personality in the time since the lift doors had opened on us, but that was the least of my concerns at the time.

"If you're willing to put your life on the line for your employee's, by all means, have at it," I told him. "If, on the other hand, you are somewhat attached to your state of being, I'd suggest moving all of this off-site ASAP and bunking down somewhere safe."

Grace Grayson did not have the manpower for something like this. If this thing blew up, we were going to have to call in reinforcements. Lucky for us, we had a few aces up our sleeves after our days in special ops.

"I see," Duncan said, his eyes darting between me and Raegan like it meant something. "Well, we can do that, certainly–"

"You'll need to reroute all traffic…" I paused and ignored Raegan's sudden interest in me. I cleared my throat. "You'll need to cover your tracks in getting back into the company servers."

Duncan nodded. "Between us, we can set that up."

I held my tongue. Any decent IT department would already have that set up. Any decent IT department would have proxy servers hiding all traffic in and out of Olafson International to private residences. It was just a no-brainer. Or, it should have been.

But I wasn't supposed to know that stuff. Olafson

didn't want tech nerd security detail. He wanted the hardened ex-military, keep their mouth shut and look imposing security detail.

"Good," was all I said. "Get the security feeds up. I need to speak to Olafson. Can you lock this level off?"

Duncan blinked at me and Jackson frowned in thought.

"You mean so no one can access it?" Raegan asked.

I nodded. "Can you block key cards from certain floors from here?"

"We're…" she started slowly, "not supposed to be able to, but I can…"

Duncan looked like he was trying very hard not to smile. "You said you'd closed off that access, Raegan."

He sounded like the teacher who knows they're supposed to tell you off but secretly think it's hilarious that you managed to hack into the vice-principal's computer and make it play heavy metal music at the highest volume every time they turned it on. Not that I knew anyone who did that at school. Twice.

"I may have left a door," she said, feigning apology.

"Use it. Block access to anyone but me until I get back," I told her and she nodded.

Short of taking her everywhere with me, this was the next best solution.

I walked out and pushed the 'up' button on the lift.

Once inside with the doors closed, I sighed and relaxed for a moment.

"This is definitely a two-person job," I muttered. "I don't know how those fuckers do it."

And I didn't. How did Chaos and Hawk and Rollie and Tank do this on the regular? I supposed most of their jobs were more like crowd control. Immediate threats in a certain vicinity we'd spent weeks vetting. Protection detail. There were the status jobs – hire us to accompany them to some do so they looked rich and important – but they were a walk in the park.

I didn't sign on for much in particular when Chaos and Hawk approached the team about going into private security. I was facing life without the overprotective, annoying, extroverts who'd against my will adopted my introverted arse. Chaos and Hawk wanted me to be their resident nerd and I jumped. No questions. I moved to Adelaide for them. I knew I'd do whatever the job required.

At the time, the job required nothing but me sitting in

the office behind my computer and ignoring the wider world. So, while I didn't sign up for anything specific, I definitely didn't sign up for being the only guy in the field on a job where someone's life was legitimately in danger.

I was used to running surveillance, checking security cameras and building schematics for weak points that posed some risk to whoever was on bodyguard duty. I was used to looking for threats that we could anticipate within a small window. That was very different than this almost witness protection detail I had going on where any attack wouldn't just be planned but could be at any random time or place.

Either Chaos knew something I didn't, or this whole thing was utterly implausible and could only end very badly.

9
Raegan

Nico was at battle stations. Like 'the Empire had just dropped a star destroyer out of hyperspace' battle stations.

"How did they find her?" he asked into the phone. "No. I haven't found anything. No one fucking has. Any luck with your contacts?"

Oh, the Grace Grayson boys had contacts!

I didn't know why that surprised me really. It made sense. I was still under the assumption that they'd all served hard time as some kind of international super spies or something. And I didn't really care to be told otherwise.

Nico sighed heavily like he was holding back some less favourable words. "Yes. It is possible," he said stiltedly. "I am aware, thank you."

He was pacing. Something he'd done a lot of in the hours since we'd got home again that morning. He'd disappeared up to Mr Olafson's office, spent a good hour or so up there, come back down to enforce our lockdown procedure, then whisked me off home.

I had to keep stopping myself from peeking out the front windows to see if the hit men were descending on the house like some rabid zombie swarm. Nothing yet, I was pleased to report.

"I am done with his shit," Nico growled into the phone and I told myself it did nothing to me. "Tell him I'm coming over there and I'm gonna fuc–"

Nico looked over and saw me watching him. He drew himself up and indifference slammed into place. I enjoyed watching him on the phone, he seemed to actually have a personality. A personality that I definitely wanted to know more about.

I was also intrigued as to the dynamics of his team. He'd been on and off the phone with various members all day, organising supplies and trading information. I felt like it was a whole lot of fuss for little old me. The whole situation was completely surreal.

"I will talk to you later," he said. A pause. "Not you,

dipshit. You can fuck right off." Another pause. "Rollie, I fucking swear…" He sighed and pinched the bridge of his nose. "Yeah, all right. You're the boss, Chaos. O L…" He looked at me. "Nico out." And hung up.

Now he'd said them, I recognised the names as being ones I'd heard floated around the office at Christmas parties the team attended. They were weird and it bugged me I couldn't remember the other two.

"So, your boss is Chaos. Then there's a Rollie and…?" I pressed.

"Hawk and Tank," he said. I couldn't tell if it was grudging or if he secretly wanted to divulge his whole life story to me.

"So, everyone in your team has a code name. Were you all super spies or something?"

He gave a single nod as his fingers danced across his phone screen. "Sort of. We met in special forces."

My mouth dropped open. I hadn't actually expected that. Then something else hit me.

"Aren't the Aussie special forces supposed to be like the best in the world?" I asked.

He shrugged, but in the way the guy just crowned world champion tries to seem humble. That or he was actually that pragmatic about it. "We've worked with some pretty good guys."

"No. But, I honestly heard they were like the best."

I had. I didn't remember where or if the source was reputable. But word on the street was that the Australian Special forces were good. Like 'train other countries' special forces' good.

He shrugged again. "Don't know what to tell you. We hold our own."

Another thing hit me. That was twice he'd almost said something other than 'Nico' when he was signing off or whatever spies called ending a communication. "If your whole team have codenames, that must mean you have one, too…"

His expression grew slightly more squirrely.

"Ha!" I exclaimed. I knew it. "That's a yes. What is it?"

He frowned. "It's need to know."

"Oh, trust me. I need to know."

He looked at me in one-part exasperation and one-part bordering on naughty. "Trust me. You don't."

"Okay. Now I really need to know."

His look was hooded, from the corner of his eyes. It

sent a zing through me. It was a different kind of zing than me just looking at him and my brain heading right for the gutter. This was a mutual interest, mutual mind-in-gutter-situation zing. I didn't know a lot about the way guys' brains worked, but I knew when one of those happened.

Then the moment was gone as he shook his head. "You don't."

Instead of risking some more zings, I gave up on it. For now. "Okay." I shrugged.

I sat on the couch and snuck looks at him as he kept pacing and checking his phone.

When the doorbell rang, he looked at me quickly.

"Expecting someone?" he asked.

I shook my head.

"Stay there."

He strode off up the hall. After a few moments, I heard him say, "State your business."

A few more minutes went by and I was sorely tempted to stick my head around the door and see what was going on. But I'd been told to stay put, and put was where I was going to stay.

Finally, Nico came back down carrying a box.

"Oh, frak!" I laughed. "I forgot about the groceries."

Nico looked like he wasn't super impressed about it, but he didn't berate me for it. "How long did you shop for?" he asked me.

I shrugged. "I meal-planned the week. Same as usual. Why?"

Nico put the box on the dining table and, before heading back up the hall, said, "Hopefully that's enough."

On that ominous bombshell, I hopped up and started putting the shopping away. While I was doing that, Nico brought another box in and put it next to the first one, then went back to his computer.

He looked worried. I'd have said he looked tense, but that had pretty much been who he was as a person since we'd met.

We went about our separate nights until he went to make a coffee after dinner.

I leant against the counter next to him. Sure, I didn't have to stop so close to him. That had been totally unnecessary. But I was still excited about the earlier zing and I was interested to see if that had been a one-time thing or not.

"Will you really not tell me your codename?" I asked him.

His tongue caressed his teeth, making a little 'tsk', sucking noise. "You might take it the wrong way."

Colour me even more intrigued. "How could I take it the wrong way?"

He licked his spoon as his eyes found mine and I had a little swoon. I could have sworn his body swayed towards mine as his eyes raked down and up my body. When they found my eyes again, there was a heat in them that I liked. More than liked. Wanted. Needed. The man was the epitome of suits, but I was quite convinced that I needed him.

"Women tend to."

Oh, ho! If I didn't find out what his codename was, I was going to burst.

Unfortunately, there was no getting it out of him that night.

****

The next day, while I was pretending to work remotely, a couple of the other guys from Grace Grayson turned up with more gear.

I didn't know who they were, but I recognised their faces. They were bigger built than Nico. Bulkier. They were both handsome men but, unlike their colleague, they didn't do anything for me. One of them was taller than Nico and one was shorter.

The taller one was in a suit like Nico's; dark grey, black tie, white shirt. His hair was almost black, his eyes a rich brown.

The shorter one was in black suit pants and a tucked in black t-shirt. His auburn hair was swept back, his green eyes shining mischievously. I smiled just looking at him.

"Miss Lane," the taller one said. "I'm Kit Grayson, this is Ryder Andrews."

"Pfft," said Ryder with a cheeky grin and holding his hand out. "Call me Rollie."

I nodded as I shook his hand. "Rollie it is. You're the one who enjoys antagonising Nico?"

"We all enjoy antagonising Nico," he said with a wink, then threw a look to the man in question.

"Rollie," Kit's voice was humoured warning. "Given this request, I'd be very careful what your next words are."

"What request?" I asked.

He held up a box.

"A coffee machine?" I looked to Nico with a wry smile. "I know you think my coffee's shit, but…"

Nico shook his shoulders out, but it was Kit who answered, "Nico's very particular about his coffee. He also needs it to function like a normal human being, so we thought we'd be doing you a favour more than him by bringing it."

I smiled at Kit. "Look, I'll take it. I've been meaning to get one of those bad boys since I moved in. Pop it on the table?"

Kit nodded and headed for the back.

I looked between him and Rollie and Nico, who were already in conversation about what else had been brought, wondering what I was supposed to do.

"Miss Lane, could you show me the back?" Kit called.

"Uh, yep. Yeah. I can do that," I said as I hurried to join him.

I threw one look back to Nico and Rollie. Rollie was grinning widely like he'd heard the best joke. Nico looked like thunder and I worried they were going to go to battle right there in my hallway.

I showed Kit around the backyard. When we came in, we found Rollie and Nico bent over Nico's computer.

"Looks good," Kit said and the other two looked up.

Nico picked up a tablet and went to talk to Chaos about stuff, which left me with Rollie.

"You settling okay with a 24/7 bodyguard?" Rollie asked with a warm smile.

I shrugged. "I guess so. It's a bit weird."

"Having security in general? Or having that particular security?"

"Both?"

Rollie laughed. "Fair. Nico's…an acquired taste."

"My best friend says that about me, too."

Who did not know I had a security guard following me around, or that I was on lockdown at home. As far as she knew, my life was as mundane and boring; I was just having some time to myself instead of going out. Luckily for me, that wasn't out of the ordinary and I'd done the mandatory health check so I was good for another week at least.

"Ah, you two must get on great!" Rollie said.

"Eh, we're all right."

We stood around for a quiet moment, before I

wondered if I could get answers out of him. He seemed nice. Forthcoming. Maybe he'd tell me what I wanted to know.

"Can I ask you something?"

He nodded. "Shoot."

"If you're Rollie, who does that make Kit?" I asked him.

Rollie looked at Kit. "Ah, that would be our esteemed leader Chaos."

"And that would make Nico…?" I tried.

Rollie sniggered. "Oh, ho. So, he hasn't told you?"

"He hasn't told me very much of anything. He said it was need to know."

Rollie rubbed his thumb over his chin. "Did he now?"

I nodded.

"I mean, he's basically moved in with you. I think we could call that need to know. Don't you think, Chaos?"

Kit looked back to us and there was more humoured warning on his face.

"Rollie…"

"What?" He held his hands up, the picture of innocence. "The woman asked me a question. Who am I to disappoint?"

I was sure Kit rolled his eyes. "I'm not saving you this time."

Rollie paused for a moment. Then seemed to make a decision. He shrugged as though he could live with that.

"O Lord," Rollie told me.

My mind didn't so much go blank as it was filled with a variety of possibilities.

"It's what now?" I asked.

"O Lord," Rollie repeated.

"It's not what it sounds like," Nico growled.

"Shame that," I heard myself say.

Rollie chuckled. "A sentiment shared by–"

Nico threw one of my cushions at him. "Enough out of you."

"What?" Rollie laughed.

I decided I quite liked Rollie. He seemed like a fun guy. He was the sort of guy I could hang out with at the pub, have a few drinks with, and come up with funny stories about the people we saw.

As much as I liked Rollie, I was hung up on this O Lord business.

I liked the sound of that. A lot. I didn't care one whit whether it was what it sounded like. I chose to fantasise it was, and I had a very good time in the fantasy land I created in my head.

So, I was a bit useless for the rest of Kit and Rollie's visit, and for a good while after. I used my distractedness as an excuse to at least sit at my desk and pretend to be working. Eventually even I couldn't pretend any longer.

I decided to try setting up the coffee machine. But I was just a little too short to reach, so Nico came to help me and we found ourselves with our arms interwoven and our faces right next to each other.

"It's honestly not what it sounds like," Nico told me.

I nodded. "Okay."

"It's short for Overlord."

I nodded again. "Okay."

"Because I... Not because I'm good at... As far as they know..." he cleared his throat. "It's not what it sounds like."

I nodded yet again. "Okay."

There were a couple of heartbeats there where I thought we were about to kiss.

Sure, I was still hung up on the whole O Lord thing, but I told myself I wasn't quite so shallow that that's all it was.

Nico was looking into my eyes and I was looking into his and the moment was charged. My whole skin felt like it had broken out in goosebumps. I took a shallow breath and licked my lip.

Neither of us moved forward, so I cleared my throat.

"Shall we give this a whirl?"

He blinked. "What?"

I pulled away quickly. "The coffee machine. Shall we…? Not…" I laughed self-consciously. "I didn't mean…"

He nodded. "Okay."

10
Nico

Of course Chaos had to have brought Rollie. And, of course, Raegan had to have got along with him swimmingly. It was disturbing just how similar those two were. They were definitely the kids the teacher separated at the back of the classroom. I was inordinately relieved when Chaos finally took him away again.

If it wasn't for him, I wouldn't have almost kissed her the night before.

At least, that's what I was going to tell myself.

Naturally, she assumed O Lord meant I was good at giving orgasms. Not that a fella didn't do his best, and all evidence pointed to my best was more than enough, but Rollie's revelation had clearly messed with whatever tenuous dynamic Raegan and I had created. Now it was super-charged with something more amorous than friendly. If it could have been called friendly in the first place.

It could have all just been me. My lack of social skills leant themselves to me reading situations incorrectly. On this occasion though, I did wonder if I was reading it perfectly fine.

In her eyes, I'd been the strong, silent, alpha jarhead. Add to that the nickname O Lord and it made for one very definite mental picture of me. The expectation of which wasn't helping me look at her in a purely professional way.

Outwardly, nothing had changed. She was still just in her usual comfortable combo. That day it was yoga pants with a lightsaber up the leg and a t-shirt that mixed 'Cowboy Bebop' with that famous Beatles album cover. The road with the crosswalk.

There was a part of me that wanted to see her every morning for forever, just so I could see what nerdy reference she'd be displaying that day. The way she was going, I bet she'd have one for every day of the month at least. I wondered if she picked them based on her mood that day or if she pulled them at random.

When it came to shirts, I was a random puller. Aside

from the fact that I was very rarely awake enough to know what I was doing first thing in the morning, the team had no idea what most of them meant.

"Doing anything interesting?" I heard her ask me.

I looked up and saw her hovering. "The team is pooling information to see what the…" I paused, without knowing who they were, knowing what to call them was difficult.

"The baddies?" she suggested.

I gave a blink and a shrug. "Sure. We're trying to determine what they know."

"Oh, Hans, are we the baddies?" she asked me with a laugh, and I looked up in confusion.

Had she hit her head? Was this whole situation messing her up more than I'd realised?

"Are we the…?" She looked at me. "You know?"

I shook my head. "No."

"Mitchell and Webb."

"Still a no."

She sighed and pulled out her phone. Her fingers moved across the screen deftly and smoothly. God that was gorgeous, the confidence with which she handled tech. As I thought that, I realised that it wasn't rare anymore, but I still liked it. Maybe I just liked it because it was her.

After a few moments, she flipped her phone to face me and hit play on a video.

Less than three minutes later, I knew what she was talking about. It was pretty funny.

"Now you know?" she sassed.

I nodded and managed not to smile despite myself. "Yes."

She gave me a wide smile as she gave a single nod. "Good."

"I'm getting another coffee. Want one?"

"Always."

She laughed. "Okay, Snape," she teased,

If only she knew that that was who I thought about every time anyone said that anymore as well. I hadn't said it meaning literally that I always want coffee. Although that was true. I had actually intended it with all the nuances behind Snape's words. Like his love for Lily, I would always be true to coffee. It was just how it was.

Not that I was going to say or do anything more than get back to my surveillance feeds and surreptitiously be working on the Ultiron upgrade when she wasn't looking.

We passed the rest of the day in our own worlds, her in the study, me alternating between patrolling, checking in with the team, checking in with Olafson and his on-site security, wading through the data we had so far, and trying to get as much of my normal work done as possible.

Raegan and I only saw each other whenever the topic of coffee was mentioned, and I told myself it was for the best. The last thing I needed was to be thinking about kissing her. It wasn't the first time that I'd noted if I was too busy mooning over her then someone could die. The fact that the someone in this situation would be her made it all the more easy to put kissing her out of my mind.

Mostly.

She finished her work before me, announcing to the house at large that she didn't get paid for overtime, and plonked herself down on the couch. She turned on a game, headset on, and I tried not to spend too much time watching it.

It was during this I heard her laugh to herself, "May the force be with you," as she totally decimated her opponent.

There was a pause until she said, "Geek? Nerd. Thank

you." Another pause. "The difference? Basically, personal preference. Nerds often tend to be more fandom-oriented. Where your average geek generally picks one area to be obsessional about, nerds tend to obsess over everything. We overlap in the gaming sectors, but the nerds are more likely to be the ones programming. But, again, personal preference. Google us and you'll get a whole lot of different definitions. Those are mine."

It was lucky she was facing away from me at that point, because I was staring at the back of her head like it held all the answers to the universe and they had, in fact, not come out to 42 after all.

"Same," she said and I heard the smile in her voice. "Good game."

She barked a laugh as she closed the game. "Queen Rage. Now there's a tag. Ha! Imagine if you gamed," she called and I realised it was directed to me. "O Lord and Queen Rage. That'd be a team that'd raise some eyebrows."

That it would. But with her love for all things nerdy, I thought Lois suited her far better. Lois. Fitting considering my first impression of her had been my own personal kryptonite. As in Lois Lane. Because her last name was Lane.

Why am I explaining this to myself?

Not that I had a split-second vision of who her Superman might be.

"You don't game, do you?" she asked, putting a thankful stop to that.

I shrugged. "Not for a while." If a while was about a week. Coincidentally about the amount of time I'd been on round the clock detail.

"Want to learn?"

It was tempting to game with her, but I had a job to do. Besides, I wasn't the kind of guy to pretend I couldn't game just to play a role or appease a woman's ego. No. Best I just steer clear of gaming around her altogether.

I shook my head. "I've got a few things to do."

"Yeah, me too," she sighed heavily. "I should do something about food. I'd suggest tomorrow, but I suppose Duncan will notice if I do *nothing* for the next week, huh?"

"You seemed to be doing an awful lot of nothing all day," I commented dryly as I fiddled with an annoying piece of code.

"Oh, that's my specialty," she told me. "I can look like I'm elbow deep in binary, but in actual fact, I've tweaked a single line and am daydreaming about 1970s Harrison Ford."

I was only half-listening so it took me a while to realise what she'd just said. I looked at her over my laptop screen.

"1970s Harrison Ford?" I couldn't stop myself asking.

She nodded. "Oh yeah. Don't know what is it about him, but me likey."

"It's probably just the pants," I said absently as I went back to my coding.

"What?" she asked.

That had perhaps been too much information. "What?"

"What do you know about 1970s Harrison Ford's pants?" She sounded like she thought she was on the precipice of uncovering something juicy.

I shrugged and sighed. "Nothing," I told her. Which was semi-true. I'd always been drawn to his holster myself. The one for the blaster, that is.

"No. Not nothing."

I looked at her again and found her leaning over the

back of the couch towards me.

"Have you got nerd brothers or sisters I should know about?"

I scoffed as I went back to my work. "Trix is anything but a nerd."

"So, you do have a family? You didn't just spawn all buff and gorgeous and mysterious, then?"

My eyes were drawn to her again. "What?" spluttered out of my mouth.

She sighed heavily like I'd disappointed her. "Spawn. It's when you…like materialise in a game. Happens at the beginning and, if you've got your settings on, any time you die. Spawn point is sacred, my man."

I knew what spawning was. I knew the spawn point was sacred. I wasn't questioning that. It was the buff and gorgeous and mysterious I was hung up on. The spawn point thing was a good enough cover.

I gave her a nod. "Right. Of course."

Another dramatic sigh. "That laptop is wasted on you, Nico– What even is Nico short for?" She suddenly changed the subject.

"Nicolas," I told her without thinking.

And this is what attraction did to a trained brain.

Proper attraction. The kind where you forget yourself, your job, your mission. At least, this is what attraction did to a trained brain who was only half paying attention because it was trying to finish coding the new Ultiron security system.

Note to self – don't let bad guys distract me with coding as an intel extraction method.

It's always good to know one's weaknesses.

"Hm…" she started. "Nicolas Daniels. Why does that sound familiar?"

If I hadn't heard of her before this job, I doubted any of my shenanigans were on her radar. Had they been, I doubted she could link Nicolas Daniels to them anyway.

"My Olafson International keycard used my full name," I reminded her.

"Oh, yeah," she mused. "Huh. My memory's worse than I thought."

"Who needs memory when you've got RAM," I heard myself say, then froze.

She spluttered a laugh and all her attention was back on me. "What did you just say?"

Okay, it was time to stop trying to multi-task.

It was like my subconscious wanted her to know

everything about me. It seemed hellbent on divulging every part of me, whether I was highly trained or not. True, my highly-trained wasn't quite as high as the rest of the team because I was the resident nerd back at base whispering sweet nothings in their ears – like safe combinations. I was better trained to talk to computers than I was humans. Likewise, I was better trained to pry secrets from computers, not hide them from people.

I shrugged her interest off. "Friend of mine says it a lot." I was my own friend, right?

"This the same friend who knows anything about 1970s Harrison Ford's pants?" she asked, suspicion in her tone.

I closed my laptop and stood up. "Sure."

"Figures you'd end a conversation just when it got interesting," she said ruefully.

All right. I was interested. "Why?"

She gave me a super sexy, adorable, cheeky grin. "Super spies aren't known for spilling their guts, 'specially to someone they just met. I could be an enemy spy for all you know."

She couldn't. I'd been in her home and work systems. Unless she was ten times better than even the Pillock gave her credit for, there was no way she was a spy. By a lot of people's definitions – including my own – there was no way I was a super spy either.

"No. But they do have patrol to do."

Her sigh was the most dramatic one to date. "Fine!" As she hauled herself off the couch, she said, "I'll get started on dinner."

****

After dinner and a movie, Raegan had gone to bed and I was in desperate need of a shower. I tended to be in desperate need of a shower when there was a woman I wanted but shouldn't have. I'd learnt that in the past week.

I liked her shower. It was bigger and had better water pressure than mine.

After I was done, I wrapped the towel around my waist and ran my hand through my hair. As I turned, the bathroom door opened and Raegan walked right into me. My arms went to her instinctively as we both found our footing.

"Oh, frak!" she squealed. "Sorry!"

I was looking at her and she was looking at me.

She breathed out quickly. Her hand on my chest softened and I felt my heartbeat quicken. She was hard up against my naked chest and I was very aware there were a couple of water droplets on it still. I was also very aware that she was in a very thin bathrobe she was holding together as though it was going to fall apart if she didn't.

I had to answer her. "No. I'm sorry."

"For being in here half naked in prime position for me to run into you because I wasn't thinking?"

I nodded. "That."

There was a smile in her eyes as she bit her lip. "I should really let you finish up."

I nodded again.

Neither of us moved.

Everything in me wanted to kiss her.

I wasn't fussed about the whole her being a client thing. I wasn't thinking about the fact that, if I kissed her, we'd have to deal with the fallout of that while I was still on detail for the foreseeable future and how awkward that might be. I wasn't thinking about the fact that I hadn't thought about anything other than one and done for years.

I didn't care she was attracted to a persona I couldn't keep up indefinitely if I did kiss her. I conveniently forgot the real me didn't know how to talk to people.

All I could think about was kissing her.

But I was frozen in place.

I was sure my heartbeat was so loud that she could hear it.

I was convinced my heart was about to go all cartoon on me and start beating out of my chest.

Or maybe my eyes were just going to pop out of my head and turn into hearts.

Neither persona knew what to do with the feelings she elicited in me.

The suave, suited Nico would have picked her up deftly, pressed her against the glass of the shower screen and given her a kiss to ruin her for all men. It would have been easy. It would have been smooth. It would be pure heat. He'd have had her moaning his name in minutes and pushed her away – physically and emotionally – once they were done.

Future ruined.

The arrogant, socially inept Nico would have crushed his lips to her in something close to desperation.

Everything he couldn't say with words would be in that kiss. Then he'd overthink everything that came next and probably accidentally smoosh his nose on her glasses while their teeth crashed together and she'd have no interest in a second try.

Moment ruined.

"Ah…" I made a noise that was part rough chuckle and part trying to release phlegm stuck in your throat as I stepped away from her. I cleared my throat and tried again. "I shouldn't keep you. I can get dressed in the spare room."

"No," she breathed. He eyes didn't seem to know where to focus. "That's fine. I will… Go. I will go."

She backed out quickly, giving me a once over with hungry eyes and a smile that was sweetly at odds, then closed the door.

I leant on the sink vanity and gave myself a good hard look in the mirror.

"What the fuck is wrong with you?" I asked my reflection.

That guy didn't seem to know any more than I did.

I hurriedly got dressed, bundled up my shit and hightailed it out of there.

"Done," I called.

"Thanks," I heard from her room.

I didn't see her for the rest of the night, and I felt like that was probably for the best.

11
Raegan

Oh. My. God.

Nico out of a suit was just as tantalising as Nico in a suit. No. Strike that. More tantalising. Way better. A perfect level of buff tautness without being overly chunky. And I'd had not only my hands but my face ALL over it.

Ugh.

He was warm and firm, but his skin was soft and I just wanted to run my hands over his body for hours. I mean everywhere. The thought distracted me all night and we weren't even in the same room.

Lying in bed on Thursday morning, I thought about touching his body. Everywhere. Basking in that just post-waking up glow where you're still all warm and cosy and have yet to remember you have a day of work ahead of you, I thought about it. No one was there to see the goofy smile on my face it gave me. No one was there to chastise me for wanting a guy I shouldn't want, at least until after his job was done. And no one was there to remind me there was no reason he'd be interested in my goofy butt.

So, I enjoyed it.

But all good things must come to an end, and no work days end unless you start them.

I got up to find him pacing the backyard on the phone. He'd been on the phone a lot over the last couple of days. As far as I could tell, for all their intel reports, there wasn't a lot of anything coming up.

"They have to be either *the* worst or *the* best bad guys in the history of forever," I muttered to myself as I shuffled over to the coffee machine.

I'll admit, I had no idea how I'd lived without one before, or how I was going to manage after Nico's job was done. Those little pods were a million times better than instant coffee and they were right there, in my house, all just begging to be drunk.

What went really well with coffee? Toast, of course.

But naturally my toaster was a thousand years old. As I was struggling with it for the umpteenth time in my life,

Nico came back in.

I heard him mumble and I was sure it was, "Frakking toaster."

I whirled around, piece of bread in my hand brandishing like a really awful weapon or an equally awful fan. "What?" Because no way did that delicious, suited jarhead know anything about *Battlestar*.

Because if he did, I was officially in love. But he didn't because…well, look at him. I was looking at him and I was half in love with him as he was.

"Fucking toaster," he said more clearly.

My eyes narrowed on him, but he was as unwavering under my scrutiny as he had been since we'd met. Guy was like a marble statue come to life, except he was only half alive and whoever had spelled him alive had forgotten to give him more than two emotions; concerned and angry.

I further brandished my bread at him. "Okay, then."

Concern marred his features for a moment, but like he was worried about my mental state. I didn't blame him. I was still brandishing a slice of bread at him. I was definitely not getting any cheevos for my stealth ninja moves or secret assassin skills. Which just made me want to get back to *Assassin's Creed*…

Nico nodded once. "Okay."

"Okay," was all I could think of to say before I went back to fighting with the toaster.

Once I'd bested my mighty foe, I made off to the study with the spoils of my victory. Namely a coffee, two pieces of Vegemite toast and two pieces of Nutella toast – one must have mains and dessert for a good balanced breakfast.

I turned on my computer and logged into the remote work server.

In the last week, I'd been sorely tempted to go digging for more information. After all, I was all for helping get my life back to normal. Two things were holding me back. Firstly, there was the part of me who was terrified what I might stumble on and be incredibly unequipped to deal with. Secondly, the sooner my life was out of danger, the sooner I'd never see Nico again.

Granted, the second thing was slightly less important than my personal health, but the two combined into a powerful incentive to let the professionals handle the job.

I joked that if I hadn't gone into IT, I'd probably have tried breaking into the FBI and hoped they'd give me a job. Aside from the fact I doubted the FBI hired Australian citizens and I didn't much care about the Australian equivalent, I was actually the sort of person who tried to keep their nose out of trouble. While I'd been told repeatedly that I was good enough to do a lot of naughty things, I kept my toe on the side of cheeky – where the only reprimand was a slap on the wrist and banishment from a portal.

As I ate my toast and swung around on my desk chair, I looked around my study to avoid doing any real work.

Janice was having problems with her email. Again. *I just hope she got her Thrusting Swan...*

Mike up on four had a bunch of corrupted files.

Geoff on six couldn't get the projector in Conference Room 2 working.

Linda on nine, via Nicky on fifth, thought her whole computer was broken.

Rochelle at the front desk was having problems syncing her calendar.

Fatima on first was having a problem with the charging port on her phone. *So not my problem.*

And that was just the emails that had come through between eight and eight-thirty.

"It's going to be a long day," I muttered to myself around my mouthful of toast.

As it turned out, it wasn't that long a day because I realised my productivity was hampered by the state of the cabling in my study. And by that I mean I got bored trying to troubleshoot the projector issue remotely.

It became clear to me quite quickly that I wasn't going to get anymore work done until the cables had been sorted out. So, I gave up, thanked whatever god was in charge of getting me dressed in the morning that yoga pants had become the norm, and climbed up onto my desk.

In hindsight, putting the router on top of my bookshelf had been a brilliant and stupid idea. But then, putting the NBN box at the top of the wall also seemed a brilliant and stupid idea.

Half an hour later, I had most of the study unplugged and was in the process of trying to untangle cables.

"What are you doing?" I heard Nico ask.

I turned as best as my weird contortion would allow me. "I'm organising my cables," I told him.

He looked at me like he was pretty sure I was crazy. "Do you…? Do you need a hand?"

I pulled myself back to the posture God had intended for me and huffed a piece of hair out of my eye. "I've told you before this princess rescues herself."

He leant on the doorframe and it did pleasant wibbly wobbly things to my insides.

He rubbed a thumb over his chin before he crossed his arms and said, "Seems to me I've failed my mission if I'm running you to the emergency room after something as mundane as a cabling accident."

He had a good point.

"Your arms *are* longer than mine," I said slowly, pretending that was why I was ogling him shamelessly.

"Just tell me what you want."

"Oh, good lord," I murmured to myself. "Breath." I want to say I didn't fan myself a little, but I did. "I want you…"

He blinked and I realised I'd just stopped.

Freudian slip anyone?

"I want you to help me secure these better," I said, hoping that the faster I said it the quicker we could move on from that verbal diarrhea. "Please."

He nodded. "Okay."

I bustled about, selecting the right cable and finding

the cable clips I'd bought when I'd moved in with the intent to do exactly this.

"Right. Can you hold these there and I'll just…?"

I put the footstool in place and climbed up onto it.

"All right," I said, more to myself than anyone else. "Now, if I just…" I secured the cable and, quite pleased with myself, turned to find myself encircled by his arms and our noses millimetres apart. "Oh. Hi…" I breathed like I'd forgotten how to talk.

To be fair, I was mesmerised by his eyes.

I wanted to say this had been a carefully orchestrated moment, set up for the express purpose of me flirting with him. I wished I was that clever. Clearly, I was also not being awarded any cheevos for battle strategy.

"What?" he asked, a slight smirk in his eyes.

"What, what?"

"You said something about cheevos for battle strategy."

I huffed a laugh, realised we were far too close to be doing such a thing and snapped my mouth shut until I got control over myself.

"Right. Yeah. No. Achievements. Like in games. Cheevos. You know?"

He gave a single nod. "Gotcha."

Oh, he had me. Hook, line and sinker.

My laugh was way more self-conscious than I'd intended it. "Because I didn't… I mean, this whole… Not on purpose. Not that it's not very nice in your… I should probably stop talking now."

His eyebrow quirked and my stomach somehow managed to skip a beat.

"Should you?"

"Shouldn't I?" came out so high-pitched I was surprised humans could hear it. I sounded like Thor before his mighty balls dropped.

This was the third time now I'd been convinced there was kissing right around the corner. And I was indeed keeping score.

This was the third time we'd come face to face – or chest – and there had been definite vibes, a moment. I didn't know if the thing holding one or both of us back had been fear, nerves, halitosis, or a big fat lot of hallucinating on my part and disinterest on his.

It felt so real to me that I was sure I had to be going insane if it was all one-sided.

"Okay," I breathed when neither of us moved forward.

"Am I crazy, or is there a vibe here, Mabo?" The Aussie in me came out big with that old reference.

"Vibe?" he asked.

To the untrained ear, he sounded clueless, or perhaps just not interested.

It was me. I was the untrained ear.

I needed answers.

"Between us. Am I making up this…" I waved my hand in what little space there was between our persons. "There's a…zing, right?"

He took a deep breath and licked his lip. Some primal, ancient part of me knew in my bones that he wanted to say yes, that there was just something holding him back. I had this ridiculously uncanny knowledge that there was this intangible connection between us. That something about me and him was meant to be. If that something turned out to be a one-night stand, and then supreme awkwardness while my life was still in danger, I was prepared to face the consequences.

"Okay. I'll make it easy for you," I said, looking into his eyes. "I'd really like to kiss you. So, unless you tell me you're not interested, I'm going to kiss you."

His mouth opened.

He said nothing.

His eyes narrowed for a second.

He said nothing.

He closed his mouth.

He was obviously not going to say anything.

"I know a lack of no doesn't equal consent, but I'm trying to do a cute bit here," I told him and I saw the warm humour in his eyes. "I'm going to kiss you, okay?"

A single nod. His eyes still on mine. "Okay."

My heart fluttered in my chest like it was doing a happy dance. One word had never sounded so good to me.

"Okay," I repeated, then leant forward.

He didn't pull back or try to stop me.

So far, so good.

As I got closer to him, I suddenly slow-mo freaked out and had a full three-round debate in my head about when the appropriate time to close my eyes was, and a subsequent rebuttal of where was I supposed to put my hands.

Just as I was about to decide I'd made a very big mistake and claim I was in fact as mad as he must think me, our lips met and everything felt right with the world.

Everything made sense.

It didn't matter what I did with my eyes or my hands. They just did their thing naturally. Like my body knew how to kiss him from some long-forgotten past life that had us destined.

Which was utter crap, but it sounded a whole lot better than he kissed my socks off.

I hadn't even been wearing any socks.

But had I been, he would have kissed them off.

Nico's lips were firm and soft. He tasted roasted – in the smoky, coffee sense, not the drunk off his nut sense. His hand left the top of the bookshelf behind me and came to rest on my neck as our bodies instinctively moved closer together.

I was torn between melting to a happy little puddle at his feet and throwing myself at him. That's what kind of kiss it was. It was deep and heart-achingly sweet, but like we were on the precipice of the greatest passion known to man. All we had to do was give into it.

We didn't.

As though we'd come to some unspoken agreement, we pulled away from each other gently. Nico and I looked into each other's eyes. I couldn't tell if we were asking if we should do that again or if we were agreeing to leave it there.

It must have been the latter because no one surged forward to claim the other with unrestrained desire or anything.

"You taste like chocolate," was the first thing he said.

As far as impressions I liked to leave, 'tasted like chocolate' had not been high on the list. Not that I was complaining. The guy had a bedroom voice like no other. And I didn't even think he knew he was using it. He could have told me the toilet was clogged and shit was pouring out of the sewer in that voice and I would have swooned.

"Nutella toast," was apparently my best explanation.

He took a deep breath, rested his forehead to mine for a second, the hand on my neck tightening its embrace slightly, then pulled away.

"Is that the cables all sorted?"

Were we not going to talk about how epic that kiss was? It might have been g-rated, but I definitely had not had better. Ever. There was something more in it I wanted to explore. Preferably with my tongue.

But the moment had passed, and that felt okay. I knew somehow that, if it was meant to be, we'd find another one. In the meantime, it didn't have to be awkward.

I tucked my hair behind my ear and smiled at him. "That's the cables all sorted."

"Great. Try not to get electrocuted or fall from any heights."

"Oh, you care," I teased.

He gave me a very serious look. "Of course, I care," he said.

"Right. No. Of course, you do." I nodded.

We looked at each other for another couple of heartbeats. Tension swirled around us, but it was a good kind. Finally, he just bowed his head, then went off to do whatever it was Nico actually did while he was looking all suave and sexy and mysterious.

12
Nico

Friday saw over a week that we'd been stuck together in close quarters and I was unravelling.

I could feel it.

I kept letting things slip.

And that didn't even take into account me letting my tongue slip the day before. Not just about the frakking toasters, but right into her mouth. All right. Not quite, but close enough.

That kiss, though.

There was no regretting a kiss like that.

It was one of a kind. It was special. I couldn't put my finger on why – on what it was about it – but I was pretty sure I'd remember that kiss on my deathbed.

I was walking up the hallway on my usual patrol when I heard a scream from her room. Reacting on pure instinct, I shouldered my way through the closed door – hearing another yelp – and met zero resistance.

My eyes scanned the room for danger. They came up with nothing. As in not even any obvious sign of Raegan.

"Good Baby Jesus," I heard her whistle and she finally half emerged from behind her bed. "You sure know how to make an entrance. Talk about knocking a girl off her feet. Quite literally."

I leapt over her bed unthinkingly and crouched down in front of her. While I assessed if she was hurt, I didn't pay much attention to what she was wearing. Or, rather what she wasn't.

"You're okay?" I asked, not seeing any outward sign of injury.

She nodded. "Fine. I stubbed my toe then fell off the bed when you came barging in like some diabolical white knight."

I looked into her eyes. "I thought this princess rescued herself?"

She shrugged and looked away from me as she said, "Maybe it's good for the knight's ego if the princess lets him save her once or twice."

I felt my cocky smirk play at my lips, totally unbidden.

"Oh, you *let* me save you?"

"That's right."

"From the floor?"

"The floor *is* lava."

"Which is incredibly dangerous."

"You know it. What are you going to do about it?"

This was dangerous ground we were treading, but I couldn't stop myself. I wasn't the knight in shining armour type. I wasn't even the knight in leather type. I wished I was the space cowboy type, but even that was a pass. Didn't stop me, though.

"Rescue the princess," I said to her.

I gently picked her up off the floor and that was when I actually paid attention to what she was wearing. She was back in that mighty thin bathrobe. It barely covered her body. It clung to every arch and curve, every dip of her skin. It rode up her legs and hung off her shoulder, leaving swathes of skin on display. And she looked into my eyes like she knew exactly what the whole package was doing to me, which only served to heighten the response I had to her. I liked an assertive woman.

Our eyes were glued to each other's as I slowly lowered her feet to the floor.

Tension zinged between us and I desperately wanted to act on it.

Again, in the moment, I forgot all about the consequences. I didn't care about the ramifications, and I wasn't thinking about one Nico or the other.

I was just a Nico standing in front of a Raegan, and hoping my next move wasn't unwelcome.

Because I took her cheek in one hand as the other went to her waist and I kissed her.

Let's be honest, it wasn't the world's hottest kiss right out of the gate. I was trying to be gentle, to give her space to push me away and tell me I was an idiot. She might have wanted to kiss me the day before but that did not mean she wanted to kiss me then. Even if everything I knew about that sort of thing was screaming at me that she was reciprocative.

It wasn't until she grabbed my jacket lapel, pressed against me and deepened our kiss that I felt myself breathe and my heart kick in again.

From there, I was lost to her.

She tasted like minty toothpaste.

She smelled like a garden in the middle of Spring rain.

She felt warm and soft, and her body fit into mine like

we were each other's perfect Tetris combo. Her L-piece hugged my square like we'd spent six rows setting it up.

Limbs wrapped around each other like we couldn't get close enough.

Nothing about this could ever feel wrong, circumstances be damned. It just felt right, and I didn't care that it made no sense or that I didn't know why. She was my perfect fit and I was going to let it carry me away.

Her hands roved over my body, exploring every inch she could reach. When she got to the waist of my trousers, her fingers made short work of untucking my shirt and running up my abs. She left a pleasant heated tingle everywhere she touched and I was straining against my zipper in no time.

I slid my fingers up her leg under the hem of her bathrobe, and the alarm suddenly went off on my laptop. I pulled away from her quickly. There was an apology in my eyes, but no time to voice it.

I ran out of the room and pulled up the feed on my laptop. There was a cat wandering along the fence, happy as you please. The furball clearly gave no cares that I was on high alert in there and it wasn't helping matters. There was nothing quite like being cock-blocked by a cat.

The question remained; was the apology in my eyes for starting something or stopping it?

Realising what I probably looked like, I tucked my shirt back in as I walked back to Raegan's room. By the time I got there, she was dressed and in the process of slipping her glasses on. Her fandom t-shirt of choice that day was an homage to the cancelled before its time 'Firefly' with 'Kaylee's Shiny Spacecraft Repair' written across it. The day's yoga pants had BB8 down the leg. Her hair was in a ponytail and her fringe was clipped back.

The look in her eyes told me she was taking this as seriously as I was, despite getting close to the point where it felt like all of this security was unnecessary. I wasn't going to begrudge any extra time I spent with her, though.

"All clear," I told her. "Just a cat."

I saw her visibly relax. "Oh, okay. Good. Yet another reason to hate cats," she chuckled, but there was something about it that sounded forced.

Was it the post-hook-up 'where do we go now' weirdness or was it post-'I thought it might have been murderers' weirdness?

"You don't like cats?" I asked her, trying to sound

casual and not at all like I wanted to play numerous rounds of twenty questions and find out everything about her.

She shook her head. "Dog person."

I kept my expression neutral. I was also a dog person. I didn't get cats. They were weird. Dogs loved you no matter what. They didn't care if you knew how to talk to them, so long as you did.

"Would be good security."

She smiled. "Yeah, nah. I've always liked the idea of adopting a greyhound. Utterly lazy and totally loving. I think I'd do a better job protecting it."

I shrugged. "Might be right."

We stood in silence, just looking at each other for a moment. I didn't think it was particularly awkward, but there was a lot hanging unsaid – or undone – between us. I could feel it as tangibly as I could feel the tightness of my shirt cuffs. Aside from the fact that Raegan seemed to really like the suit combo, one thing I missed about the job was my normal choice of clothes.

I envied her being able to be herself.

Not that I knew which Nico I'd be around her given the freedom to choose.

"Coffee?" I asked finally, realising that we couldn't just stand in her bedroom and make moony eyes at each other all day.

She nodded. "Sure. Want me to get it?"

I shook my head. "I can bring it in. You get to work."

She smiled, and I was man enough to admit it lit me up inside. "It's not like you're not already working."

I let myself give her a small smile in response. "My work's…different."

"I'll say," she chuckled. "You get paid just for existing. I have to, you know, actually tick things off my to-do list."

"I do slightly more than just existing, thank you."

Now she laughed. "Hey, I'm not complaining you exist. I'm quite pleased you exist. But you've got to admit that it's a little less…immediately demanding." I could tell by the look in her eyes that she was taking the piss.

Again, her similarity to Rollie hit me. Also again, I wasn't inclined to punch the stupid teasing from her face. I was somewhat inclined to kiss it off, but I was more inclined to go along with the joke. I had never been that guy, unless the joke was at one of my team's expense.

"Definitely. My job is way easier than if the servers

go down because Janice's dubious internet history introduces a trojan to the system," I said as we walked out of her bedroom.

She snorted, her eyes shining bright with humour. "Janice and her internet history. I should reinforce the firewalls on her computer and make sure that doesn't happen," she chortled.

As we paused in the doorway to her study, she gave me a suspicious look.

"What do you know about trojans?" she asked.

"Brand of condom?" I suggested and she snorted again.

"Yeah, because I need to be worried condoms are going to infiltrate our system. Ha!" she barked a laugh. "I probably should with Janice all over those online sex shops."

She continued chuckling to herself as she went into her study, seemingly distracted enough to not look too deeply into my unfiltered words. They didn't fit with her view of me or the role Olafson wanted me playing. I was nothing if not a company man, for Chaos' sake at least. He'd worked hard to build our company, and it was because of him that I enjoyed the financial freedoms I did.

So, I was determined to keep toeing the line of the ex-military, suited wanker who wouldn't even know his video card from his network card if the components were labelled.

If I was going to manage it, I was going to have to watch that part of me who kept trying to let my nerd side free. Raegan didn't seem interested in that type anyway. So, it should have made it easier to play the role.

It didn't.

She was driving me insane. My fingers itched to touch her. I had to keep balling them up to stop them fidgeting. Her kiss was all I could think about. How could I do it again? When could I do it again?

I tried telling myself she was just a job.

I knew that was a lie.

Raegan Lane was not just a job.

Just then, I wanted her more than I'd ever wanted anything else in my life. I was convinced I'd go mad if I didn't have her.

But one night wasn't an option.

Sleeping with her and never seeing her again wasn't an option.

Chaos wasn't going to let me switch assignments just because I couldn't keep it in my pants.

If I gave in to my desire for her, I knew I'd have to find some way of not being a complete dick around her after.

That still wasn't enough to stop me wanting her.

And I wasn't sure how long my determination could win out.

13
Raegan

I felt…antsy. Itchy. Restless.

Somehow in the last few hours, I'd developed a manic case of restless leg syndrome Except it seemed to be affecting my whole body. My legs kept jiggling like I was dancing to music where I sat. I had one hand on the mouse and, when the other wasn't typing, it was clicking a pen. When I wasn't clicking the pen, I was chewing on the end of it. Even my brain seemed restless, constantly jumping from one thing to another, randomly refreshing websites or my email. And all throughout, I kept stretching my neck and shifting my position in my desk chair. It was like I was suddenly super ergonomically conscious.

Coincidentally, it had also been a few hours since I'd almost pulled Nico onto my bed and begged him to have his wicked way with me. And why hadn't I? Because of a cat. A cat! I didn't know what the female equivalent of cock-blocked was – pussy-blocked seemed apt given the situation – but I'd never experienced it because of a cat.

And all I could think about was where Nico's hands had been heading when his stupid perimeter sensor had been tripped.

I leant my head on my desk and sighed.

Luckily, my phone vibrated and I told myself that it must be very important and should be checked at once. It was just an email from some random newsletter I'd signed up to forever, never opened the emails, and never unsubscribed from. As I was putting down my phone, it vibrated again and this time it was very important and should be checked at once.

> **Filmore**
> Okay. Plans for the evening. And go.
> **Mel**
> Why don't you *go* for once?
> **Filmore**
> Because I'm the odd man out and as a perfect gentleman wish not to tread of the dainty toes of

the ladies.

> **Rage**
> You, sir, are full of steaming horse shit.

Mel
She's not wrong.
Hey! She's alive!

> **Rage**
> I am alive!

Filmore
Have you almost finished that system upgrade yet?

Mel
Are you coming out tonight?

So, yeah. I might have told my friends that I'd been less chatty the last week because work had exhausted me because we were doing a massive system overhaul. I had half a mind to suggest to Duncan that we do a massive overhaul just so I didn't feel so guilty about lying to them. But what? Was I going to tell them I had a temporary live-in body guard – who, yes, happened to be sex on legs – and freak them right out? No. Easier to just not say anything.

> **Rage**
> Nah. I'm wiped. Gonna stay in, eat junk, and marathon Star Wars or

something.

Filmore
Again?

Mel
Ugh. You suck. No. You don't, but ugh. Work sucks!

Filmore
The whole adulting system sucks.

Rage
Yes. This though ^

Mel
You take care of yourself. Lots of green tea and fruit!

I rolled my eyes at Mel and her current health kick.

Rage
No, shan't. I'm going to have all the coffee and chocolate and GMOs!

Filmore
Ooo. Badass.

Mel
Some of us care what we put in our bodies. Deal with it.

Rage
Hey! I care. I care it tastes good and makes me feel good.

Filmore

Chocolate is not a suitable replacement for real companionship.

Rage

Yeah, thanks Master Obi Wan. Ruin all my self-sabotage why don't you.

Mel

snort

Filmore

And just like Anakin you're going to do whatever you fucking want and then complain it's the system that's broken and it's no fair and everyone's mean to you.

Rage

I'm not getting into this argument with you again.

Mel

Oh, don't mind me. I'm more than happy to watch.

Mel wasn't quite as nerdy as me and Filmore. She'd watch whatever we made her watch and she just enjoyed the experience. She didn't inhale everything and then argue over the smallest plot or character details for years after.

Rage
It is literally only because I don't have time.

Filmore
You're just worried I'll change your mind.

Rage
You just wish you'd thought of destroying an entire society – nay religion – for the woman you loved.

Filmore
Yeah. Because nothing says 'I love you' like murdering helpless younglings *eye roll*

I could easily have passed the time arguing with him over why it was romantic that Anakin went all dark side – it wasn't for the cookies. But I'd been dicking around for the majority of the day and it was still slightly too early to justify calling stopping now an early minute.

Rage
Okay. But I do actually have do so *some* work today.

Filmore
Fine. We'll pick this up sometime tomorrow

afternoon after the hangover's manageable.

> **Rage**
> Deal. I want pics tonight.

Mel
Or you could come with and not miss out on anything...??

> **Rage**
> Or I could stay home and veg out and *gasp* get wine drunk in my pjs!!

Filmore
I want to get wine drunk in my pjs.

Mel
No. You can't NOT come out now.

Filmore and I waited for a few seconds before she replied to herself.

Mel
Or...I could ALSO get wine drunk in my pjs?!?

Filmore
We're all getting wine drunk at our individual homes in our pjs tonight, aren't we?

> **Rage**
> Yes

Mel
Yes!
Filmore
Thank fuck. Okay. I'm going to go stare at the clock until 5 so I can get a head start on you bitches.
Mel
Damn you!

I chuckled to myself as I put my phone down and went back to trying to do some work. I hit refresh on everything and still couldn't focus.

"Coffee," I said suddenly.

It had been a while since I'd last had coffee. As in, since Nico first brought me my post-hook-up cup. I wondered if that meant he was avoiding me after our little display, or if he'd just lost track of time trying to stay focussed, like me.

I pushed my chair away from the desk – shooting a little further than intended and almost falling off my chair – and stood up. I searched around my mess of parts and pens and random paraphernalia crap for where I'd squirrelled my mug to keep it out of harm's way. I'd lost more than a few cups of coffee because I'd perched my mug precariously and elbowed it off the table.

"A ha!" I smirked, finding it hiding under my laptop.

"Caked-in goldmine!"

No wonder I couldn't focus, I hadn't even finished my one and only coffee for the day. Clearly, I was in withdrawal. Just as I was about to take the mug to get another round, I thought better of it. A new mug would let me get some flirt on.

When I walked out of the hallway, Nico was at his laptop.

"Are you sure this whole round the clock thing is totally justified?" I sighed dramatically.

Which was a legit question as well as an ice breaker. We hadn't heard any more about whether whoever had broken into Olafson International knew who I was or where I lived. There had been nothing more than instructions on what we were supposed to do. I was starting to think it was all more palaver than necessary.

He shrugged like he agreed with me, but it was what it was. "I've got orders."

That had been the wrong thing for him to say. I was going to take full advantage of it. "And do you always do what you're told?" My tone should have less suggested and more whacked him over the head with what I was thinking.

He looked up at me, his eyes calculating. He took a moment to bite his lip like he was trying to decide whether he went with it or shut me down. When he spoke, his voice implied he hadn't quite decided yet.

"Sometimes," he said slowly.

I nodded as I walked to the kitchen, putting an unnecessary swing in my hips and hoping he was paying close attention.

"Sometimes? Not a very good little soldier if you only sometimes do what you're told." I personally was very proud of my seduction voice. It was nice and low, easy. Kind of like me really.

As I got a new mug out of the cupboard, a section of skin at my waist was revealed as my shirt rode up. I looked back at him over my shoulder. As easily readable as ever, I was fairly confident I was making an impression on him.

He stood up, almost too casually, and smoothed his trousers before slowly stepping towards the kitchen.

"Who said I was a good little soldier?" he asked. He'd definitely decided he was going to go with it.

I near-on Vicar of Dibley spluttered. I managed to hold it in.

"I'm tempted to say there's nothing *little* about you," I said and had to force myself not to do a happy dance at my suaveness.

Nico lay a hand on the bench either side of me, boxing me between his arms, the bench and his body. "But…?"

I legit batted my eyes at him. "I honestly wouldn't know." I shrugged like 'oh, what a pity'.

Humour warred with desire in his eyes.

I liked being this close to him. He smelled like some crisp, clean cologne. Not musky, but not sweet. It was somehow tangy and citrus-y. Which was now just the oh-so-sexy scent I associated with Nico.

"Some might call that a shame," he said.

I felt myself bite my lip. Had I not, I would have broken out into the goofiest grin known to humankind. When I had some control over my lips, I let it go.

"I'd definitely call it a shame."

Nico's baby blues shone. In them was the perfect mix of mischief, humour, that cheeky arrogance, and a hefty case of bedroom eyes. He could have poly-morphed into a tentacled, slobbering mess and I still would have come over all ridiculous at those eyes and the way they looked at me.

I saw him smile, then he dipped his face to my neck and I felt goosebumps break out over my skin. I forced my breathing to slow as his nose skimmed barely-touching over me.

My hand went to his chest. I felt him tense like he was about to pull away so my hand fisted in his shirt, telling him to go nowhere.

Painfully slowly, he pulled away and took a step back.

Was this some kind of power play? Was he putting the ball in my court? Was he actually not interested but taking pity on the nerd girl throwing herself at him?

Whoa, Fear. You are not welcome here!

I shrugged as I slowly walked to the fridge like I was planning on continuing on with making coffee.

"You want some?" I asked. If he said no because I was utterly hideous, then I could pretend I was talking about coffee. If on the other hand he said…

"I want a lot."

…I could probably work with that.

I played it cool, nodding. "I could be into that." What was I? In Year Eight and testing out my false bravado on the playground?

Thankfully, Nico didn't get repulsed, he didn't laugh

at me like I was the comically inept seductress. He walked towards me until he was right in front of me,

His eyes locked onto mine. He walked me backwards and pressed me into the wall beside the fridge as he ran his hand up my side to grip my waist firmly. And he kissed me the way I wanted Jyn and Cassian to kiss on that beach every single time. I felt my breath leave me for a second. My stomach danced itself into knots. My mind went utterly blank of everything but him. My heart fluttered in my chest.

It was the single best kiss of my life to date.

No 'give it a second to kick in'. We both just went for it from the get-go.

His fingers trailed from my waist, down over my hip and slid tantalisingly around to cup my arse.

The man was all sex god extraordinaire. His touch was sure. His kisses confident. There wasn't a single speck of hesitation about him. He knew what he was doing and he was going to do it as well as possible.

I had never felt as wanted as I did at that particular moment. I had never felt as turned on. I'd never wanted anyone that badly.

"Is this going to be the sort of lot that goes better with

a bed or…?" I breathed as his lips trailed over my neck.

"If you want it to."

I felt myself nodding against the wall behind me. "Yeah. I… I – uh – think I'd like that." Truthfully, it was sort of difficult to think of anything with him being all handsy and sexy and distract-y.

His lips moved back to mine again and he kissed me. Hard. Passionate. Dominating.

Without our lips breaking, he picked me up and wrapped my legs around his hips and walked us to my room.

"You like it sweet or rough?" he asked me, and I was sure I was a puddle of hot mess at his feet because that was sexy.

"Oh, my God," I squeaked. "Surprise me?" was possibly the lamest thing I could have said, but it was out there now.

He only smiled and kissed me as he let my feet drop to the floor. I was almost disappointed, until I saw him start to pull his jacket off. I could quite honestly just sit on my bed and watch him undress slowly. That was a thing I could be totally into.

I was so totally into it that he was taking his shirt off

before I even started to wonder if I should be taking anything off. I caught the hem of my t-shirt in hand and froze as his shirt fell open.

I'd been so caught up in the feel and smell and whole embarrassment of the situation in the bathroom the other day that I hadn't noticed the tattoos on his body. One was a sword surrounded by stars on his right pec. The other was foreign words across his right rib.

My hand touched his pec. I thought I had questions, but they disappeared from my head as soon as I looked up into his eyes. Anything I felt inclined to know about his tattoos could wait until I wasn't in the process of getting him naked.

I pulled off my t-shirt and he dropped his shirt on the floor at our feet. His shoes were gone and he lifted me up again to lay me on the bed. Running kisses down my body, he gently pulled my pants off before grazing his fingers up my legs. With a strength I liked far too much, he pulled me down the bed a little to meet him and an undignified squeal of excitement and surprise left my person.

He nestled himself to my side, his lips finding mine again as his hand danced over my stomach. As his kiss deepened, his hand grew still, moving over to my waist and gripping it firmly. Then it was moving enticingly further south.

"Is it poor form to point out you have a lot to live up to…*O Lord*?" I teased.

"Rude." His cocky smirk warmed me in many places. As his hand slipped down my undies, his lips went to my ear and he said, "I'll *handle* any complaints personally."

I was going to reply something witty and clever, but anything remotely witty and clever flew out of my brain as his finger slid over my clit slowly and his lips pressed against my neck.

Words were of no use to us now. Lips and hands roamed. Well, my hands roamed. He was propping himself up with one arm and the other hand stayed exactly where I wanted it.

His touch was light to begin with, just the right amount of teasing and stimulation to make me crave more. His fingers circled and swayed and flicked in seemingly random patterns, each change coming just before it became too much. I held him close and, when his finger slid down to enter me, I did bite his lip. Just a little.

I felt his rough chuckle vibrate between us and nipped him again just for fun. After that, all bets were off. Nico's tongue swept into my mouth to claim me and I felt my back arch in an effort to get closer to his body. His fingers worked me deftly until I felt the delicious wave building. This wasn't the lazy tingles you could just enjoy for a while. This was the desperate for more, give me release kind.

Nico was nothing if not obliging.

No more teasing. No more seemingly random touches. His fingers worked with purpose, finding the right rhythm and pressure and keeping to it despite the way my body writhed in pleasure. My breathing came heavier, each exhale closer to a moan than a breath, until I felt myself right on that edge.

My hand gripped his back tightly as I tumbled over that glorious precipice into extreme carnal satisfaction and my orgasm crashed into me with the force of Grond at the gates of Minas Tirith.

"Oh, Nico!"

I'd never been one to scream a guy's name in utter ecstasy before. There's a first time for everything and – I hoped – we were just getting started.

He showered my body in lazy kisses as I got my breath back, not helped by the fact I was super ticklish after an orgasm and he kept making me laugh.

"Condom," I finally panted and he nodded.

As I reached over to my bedside table for one, he dealt with the rest of his clothes. By the time I was turning back to him, he was pulling me closer again.

14
Nico

I was weak.

I knew it.

She made me weak.

Instead of fighting it, instead of denying it or ignoring it or raging against it, I gave into it. Gladly. Willingly. The way Eowyn went to battle for Aragorn. The way Rose looked into the TARDIS for the Doctor. The way Leia went to Jabba for Han. I couldn't not give into her.

Her kiss sent electrifying tingles across my skin. Her touch had me hungry for more.

I didn't think. I just acted.

From the moment she asked if I always did what I was told, I was on autopilot. It was simple, it was easy, it was natural. It was scary. But I let go. There was no suave Nico. There was no nerd Nico. There was just Nico.

And I wanted to feel her come apart for me over and over again.

She handed me the condom and I made quick work of getting it on. I looked up at her and she smiled at me. This part somehow made it feel less personal than I knew it was, put a slight crimp in the frenzied romanticism of it all. But I'd willingly run into a war zone buck naked before I didn't glove up.

When I was appropriately attired, I kissed her before dragging her panties down those gorgeous legs.

All of her was gorgeous. Physically, yes. But it was more than that. Her mind was tantalising. And her eyes. They were the best bit of all. Through all my bossing and shortness with her, she'd always shown exactly what she thought of me in her eyes.

She pulled my face to hers with one hand as she drew off her glasses with the other and put them on her bedside table. I was powerless in the face of her. And I kissed her exactly like it. Like I meant it, and I did.

Raegan ran her hands over my abs, up my chest, into my hair. I felt like fire when she touched me. I felt like her touch left me with my own unique brand of armour and it made me indestructible.

Our kiss heated up as her leg wrapped around my hip and drew me closer to her.

I'd been aroused before. I'd been turned on before. I'd known an all-encompassing need to have someone before.

At least, I thought I had.

Raegan was the eternal flame and I'd put Surtur's crown in there for her.

Beautifully dominant, her hand slid between us and she in no uncertain terms told me what she wanted as she coaxed my tip to her opening. I paused, just happy to drink her in for a moment. I wanted to say I needed a moment before everything changed, but everything had already changed. What I wanted was to remember this moment, to sear it into my mind so that if – *when* – I made a mess of it, I could remember it perfectly.

Her cheeks were still rosy from her orgasm, her eyes were soft and dreamy, and she looked up at me like I was the only guy in the world. In that moment, I fell and I fell hard. Raegan might have had a thing for the suited, military Nico, but he wasn't here just now. She wanted me to surprise her? Sweet it was.

As I ran my hand up her side softly, I pressed kisses

to her neck. I loved the way she tilted to give me better access and sighed when I did that. As my hand kept exploring her body, I trailed my lips up over her cheek and claimed her lips for my own again.

She was sweet and soft, her body pressing against mine as she kissed me back. It was deep and it was slow. There was no rushing going on here. If that cat decided to make a comeback now, I was going to submit a request to Chaos to rescind the no guns policy.

We kissed and I slowly thrust into her, her hips widening to make my way easier. Her knee hugged my hip, bringing us closer together as her hands grazed down my back. I was taking my time with this one and she seemed all for it. Our bodies rocked together slowly and steadily, hands exploring, lips devouring each other hungrily.

As her breathing got more ragged, I gently pressed her leg back and slid into her more deeply. Her head fell back on the pillows and I watched her bit her lip, a contented smile playing at her lips. Her eyes opened and found mine. She smiled at me and I felt myself answering it. She took my face in her hands and brought our lips back together.

She kissed me as her orgasm built, her hands both in the back of my hair, holding our faces together. She gave the smallest little moans as she exhaled. I wasn't sure if she was trying to keep them in, or if that's just how she did.

A few more strong, hard, deep thrusts and those breathy moans became louder, more definitive expressions of pleasure. They put a serious crimp in my control and I felt my own orgasm building with hers, that familiar tingle and tightening sensation that begged me to go harder, faster.

My pace increased naturally and her body changed rhythm to match mine. Her hands gripped me harder and her soft moans became heady whimpers as I pounded her. Her head fell back again and I felt her whole body tensing around mine as she urged me on.

I very rarely did what I was told, but Raegan Lane could say jump and I wouldn't even stop to ask how high.

She came hard and I followed close behind, barely hanging on long enough to satisfy her first. I'd never felt release quite like that before. There was something far more fulfilling about it being with her. I wasn't already wondering where I'd thrown my pants before I'd even slid out of her. Unlike my usual habit of nail and bail, I had the overwhelming urge to never leave her.

I thrust into her lazily, our kisses soft and sweet once more as we let our racing hearts calm. A couple more thrusts, then it was time to deal with the condom with a tissue from beside her bed. I dropped back down next to her.

"Okay," she breathed heavily. "I have questions."

I grinned at her. "Questions?"

She nodded, looking up at the ceiling before laying her arm over her eyes. "Your tattoos?"

"What about them?"

"What do they mean?"

I looked down at my body and said a silent prayer the way I always did when I thought about them. I'd never been heavily into ink. I had nothing against tattoos, I'd just never had anything important enough to stamp it on my skin for eternity. Not until…I did.

"Back when we were in special ops, we had this commander. Terrell. Total pain in my arse, drilled me half to death. He was hard on all of us, but the others didn't have to work quite as hard. No one liked him, but then who likes their commanding officer? It's his job to be a dick." I sighed heavily, my hand going to my pec. I found Raegan had rolled to her side and her hand was laying on my chest. I rubbed it absently. "That dickhead died for us. The unit got the sword and stars to honour him. Honour his sacrifice."

She rolled over to her stomach and I tried not to shy away from the tickle when she ran her hand over the other one.

"And this one?"

I kept my eyes firmly on the ceiling. That part of me that wanted her to know all of me was in control and the rest of me was too busy basking in bliss to bother telling it to shut up.

"*Gratia de per chao*," I recited. "By the grace of chaos." I chuckled humourlessly. "We thought we were terribly clever coming up with that one. Hawk's real name is Grace. Patrick Grace. We used to joke that it was because of him that we all got home safe. Because it was by Chaos' grace – his stubborn determination – Hawk got home to his sister every single time. It pushed all of us, kept us all vigilant. The rest of us owe those wankers our lives…ten times over at least."

"Was it terrible?"

I had to look at her, at the tone in her voice. "Terrible?"

She nodded. "Whatever it was you had to do…wherever you did it."

I sighed. She lay her chin on her hand on my stomach and looked at me. My arm went around her to keep her close.

"Some of it."

"I couldn't imagine," she breathed, planting a kiss on my rib. "And then to go into security."

"I promise this is the most exciting job any of us have had since we got started," I laughed.

"So, you *all* get paid to just…exist and do nothing?"

She was teasing, but she was worth a real answer.

I shook my head. "No. They get paid to escort highfaluting society darlings to lunches and fundraisers." A semi-real answer. It wasn't the only thing they got paid to do.

"So, much like this job, then?"

I gave her a smile, but it was a sober one. "Just because we haven't seen the danger doesn't mean it isn't there."

That was a lesson we'd all learned the hard way more

than once in our special ops days. I'd been lucky not to see it upfront and personal, but live video feeds still had the power to change even an antisocial creature like myself.

"I guess that's why Mr Olafson brought in the professionals, huh?

I nodded. "Only so much the police can do without any hard proof."

She batted me gently. "Okay. I have sufficiently brought the mood down low enough. And after you managed to get it up so high before…"

She stopped to laugh and I was smiling at her.

"You had to go with a dick joke," I commented.

"I did," she agreed. "I thought it was very clever."

I pulled her on top of me and wound my arms around her. "It *was* very clever."

Her eyes widened and I knew she could feel my cock digging into her hip just the same as I could.

"Seems getting it back up isn't as difficult as I assumed," she said and her voice purred for the effect it had on me.

"With you in my arms? Of course not."

She ran her fingers through the top of my hair almost

absently. "I don't suppose you'd want to just stay in bed for the rest of the night, would you?"

"I could be into that," I said, teasing her with her previous words.

She huffed and made to roll off me, but I held her tight.

"I know. World's biggest nerd," she laughed, snuggling into me.

What I didn't say was that she was the world's most perfect nerd. I didn't say it made me more attracted to her than I'd ever been to anyone in my life. And I'd been a teenage boy once.

All I did was roll her over and kiss her until she came undone for me again. And again. Until she grabbed a condom, climbed on top of me and told me it was high time she gave the orders.

15
Raegan

Okay. Yeah. Sure. Nico had blown my mind.

I'm talking 'fuel me until the end of time' blown my mind.

But he was just so…

"Ugh," I muttered to myself and threw the blankets over my head.

Of course, I had to go and fall into bed with the guy to ruin me for all others and he be totally wrong for me in every other way.

Every.

Other.

Way.

I didn't hate being around Nico. I could deal. In the short-term.

Long-term I needed a guy who talked my talk. A guy

I could nerd out with. A guy who'd re-watch our favourite shows and movies with me constantly. A guy I could game with. A guy I could beat and wouldn't sulk. A guy who not only laughed at but understood that reference.

Nico Daniels was none of those things.

He might have started out sweet, but by the end of it? He was a beast in the sheets, true, but I needed less beast and more nerd in the streets.

It was disappointing, but it made it easier to keep my eyes and my hands to myself when I got up to find leaving my bed that morning had obviously flipped some switch in him. When I walked out to the living room, I found a return of the total, uncommunicative suited jarhead.

Oh, sure. I saw the smirk in his eyes when I said something totally hilarious, but there was no witty banter, there was no joking, there was certainly no more kissing. He oozed cocky, charming, strong-and-silent vibes. I didn't know what was worse; that it made me want to smash my keyboard over his head, or that I wanted him to do all those delectably dirty things to me over and over again.

I gave myself a right talking to. Being attracted to the cocky twat thing was unhealthy and would only lead to heartache. But. Holy. Jesus.

It might have been because I knew what he could do with that body now, but I wanted him way more than I had before I dragged him to my bed and let him have at me. All night long.

After little to report in the way of pleasantries, I sat on the couch and flicked through Netflix while scrolling through my phone. There was very little of anything that could distract me from the blazing beacon that was Nico sitting just behind me. The back of my neck prickled like his eyes were on me but, when I turned around, he was studiously watching his computer screen.

When he got up to do his usual perimeter check, my eyes followed him, and I couldn't pull them off him if I tried. He moved with this fluid precision that reminded me of some jungle cat. Not that I knew anything about jungle cats outside 'the Jungle Book' and a few random Attenborough docos.

Not for the first time, my mind envisioned him as this deadly, precise weapon, unleashed on some unsuspecting foe as he dispatched them with a combination of superior martial arts and advanced ordnance handling. That didn't help me accept that the night before might have just been one night only.

It's not like I'd never found the uber soldier attractive. I watched and read enough that I appreciated the aesthetic. D'Avin Jaqobis had his own personal room in my spank bank. But that was science fiction, fantasy. Realising that I could be into that in real life was a surprise. I guess part of me had never thought that I'd ever come across on in quiet, little old Adelaide.

By the time he was done, I was on my second coffee and we continued ignoring each other; me taking full advantage of a day off to not even pretend to do anything productive, and him looking busy on his laptop, on the phone or doing his rounds.

While I was making my fourth coffee of the day, I decided that I could use the excuse of offering him one to go outside and talk to him. I found him on the phone and pacing.

"And if this security lockdown is permanent?" I heard him asking. "I'm not trying to get out of anything," he continued. "I'm legitimately asking what I'm supposed to do about Hawk's wedding if I'm still on mission."

He didn't seem that cut up by the idea of missing out on his teammate's wedding to be honest.

"I could go with you," I offered and he whirled around to face me.

I was thankful for the note of teasing in my voice. I had been kind of joking, but I also kind of very much wanted to go out with him if that was going to be a possibility.

Nico frowned and I thought it was to me until he said in the phone, "Of course you don't mind. Well, lucky it's not up to *him* then, isn't it?" A pause as he looked me over. He licked his lip and I was sure there was heated desire in his eyes. "Feasible? I dunno. The whole thing gets less feasible the longer this goes on."

He ran a hand through his hair and went back to pacing. I watched him, still under the guise of planning to ask him if he wanted a coffee. I had to assume the conversation wasn't confidential if he wasn't actively hiding it from me. I also wanted to know if something was going to change and, if it was, was it because we'd slept together? Or was it a coincidence?

"Look," he said. "I've got what I need, but that's a decent idea. We've talked about it before. Now seems the perfect time to set it up." Another pause. "And if we get raided here? I can only do so much, Chaos." Another frown. "Yeah, well he would have done a better job." I saw him roll his eyes and give a short smirk. "Who'd have thought Tank wouldn't be able to manage." Another slight smirk. "Sounds like he's not managing if she keeps giving him the slip. And you keep telling me it doesn't hurt to be a decent human being."

He threw a look to me, his expression almost guilty for a moment.

"Yeah. Okay. Run the matrix, if this is still going on by then, we'll see if taking Raegan with me will work. I can just miss it if I have to." Pause. "I'm not smiling." He was a bit. "Of course, I don't actually want to miss it. No, I have nothing against Leah. Dude, I went to the engagement, didn't I? It's not my fault." Another eye roll. "Sure. O Lord out."

He hung up and looked at me. "Did you want something?"

My hand wrung in front of my body nervously and I didn't rightly know why they'd do such a thing. "Uh, just wanted to know if you wanted another coffee?"

His eyebrow rose. "I'm good."

I couldn't stop myself responding, "Oh, I know you are."

He looked away like he was refusing a smile. "No complaints, then?"

I gave a single nod. "You definitely lived up to your reputation, *O Lord*."

There was a flash of a smile on his face before he schooled his expression. "Good. But, uh…" He stopped, then looked at me. I didn't like the apology I thought I saw on his face. "It's not exactly protocol to…" Here he paused like he was thinking of the best way to put it. "It was irresponsible of me to let myself get distracted."

"Oh."

I was a little insulted. I tried not to be, but I was. I'd hoped I was more than a mere distraction. The way he said, I'd been a nice distraction, but nothing to write home about. And here I'd just complimented him like he'd been the best I'd ever had. He had been, but he didn't need to know that if the sentiment wasn't reciprocated.

"No," I continued. "Sure. I get that."

He ran a hand through his hair and adjusted his tie. "If they'd found you while…"

I nodded. I understood, but it was the *way* he was saying it. "No. Of course. Hands off from now." I held my hands up like that was proof.

We just stood looking at each other for a while. Finally, I couldn't' take it anymore.

"About that coffee?" I asked as a segue to going back inside.

"No. Thanks." He pointed to his phone. "I have to check in with Olafson."

I gave him a nod. "Yep. Okay. No worries."

I went back inside and was too dejected even to get another coffee. Trust me to drool all over a guy who was not only totally wrong for me but who also lost interest once he'd tried me out. I needed to vent some frustration and there were a bunch of monsters in Sanctuary that had my name on them.

16
Nico

I wasn't the first Grace Grayson team member to sleep with a client.

It was what got us the business of the high society ladies with too much money and plenty of time on their hands.

I say high society, but the number in the bank account was about the only thing that separated the truly rich from the basic middle class in Adelaide. On the outside. The rich had a few more fancy shindigs than the rest of us and spent more than necessary on their cars and houses, but they went to all the same schools, they started out in all the same jobs, they holidayed at the same (local) places. There just wasn't enough going on in the good old city of serial killers – or churches if you prefer – to truly separate us. And that was the way I liked it.

So, I wasn't the first and I wouldn't be the last to fulfil varying needs of the client. As it were. Technically, Olafson was the client but he wasn't really my type.

I *was* probably the first to sleep with a client and then basically ignore her while still on the job.

But what else was I supposed to do?

I was a complete mess inside.

On one hand, there was the Nico who could have easily got her back into bed over and over again. Problem was, I didn't just want to get her into bed over and over again. But the Nico who wanted to talk to her couldn't talk to her. I didn't know what to say. Everything I did say came out stilted and weird with that condescending arrogance responsible for this being my first – and hopefully last – time in the field. Even my superiors in basic training had said I was never going to be field material. For very good reason.

I saw the way she'd looked at me since she got up.

Yeah, I'd pulled the 'slip out of bed before she woke up' trick.

There was more confusion than regret, more question than accusation. Everything I was wanted to answer her, but how was I supposed to reconcile two Nico's, one she wanted and two who wanted her, when they were so at odds with each other?

When she'd offered to be my date – not in so many words – to Hawk and Leah's wedding, I'd wanted to jump at it. I'd wanted to say she could come with me even if I wasn't still on mission. But the way she'd offered made it sound so much more like… Not an obligation or a hardship but not something she was dying to do either.

Bert
You LIKE her!

So, yeah. I'd been texting with Bert on and off while on assignment and I not-so-accidentally let slip the whole Raegan situation. After all, she was the only person in my life I'd come even remotely close to letting in to the deeper stuff. I could be a bit more vulnerable and not feel like I was setting myself up for more teasing than I could deal with. Which was on me. The team were jokers by nature. I'd just never been very good at letting them tease me. And that wasn't even taking into account Bert was the only female influence I could turn to for insights and advice.

Nico
I do not.

Bert
Yes. You do.

It was like her saying it opened a massive set of floodgates and I started to wonder if she was right. No one else would have had that level of authority over me, but Bert wasn't just anybody.

I had a sudden flashback to the whole Chaos and Bert debacle.

Chaos had just told the whole War Room that he was in love with Bert and Hawk went mental. We'd all been blind to not see it coming. Two people living in the same house, of course they were going to fall in love.

There was a stark comparison there between them and the whole Raegan situation I chose to ignore.

But it was what Chaos had told Hawk that I thought of just then. He'd said we all deserved a little romance in our lives. That we all deserved someone who we could cuddle up to on the couch after a hard day. Whose kiss made all the horrible things we'd been through seem not so bad. Whose smile lit you up inside. In whose arms you felt worthy of love for once.

Maybe I did – or at least could – feel that way about Raegan.

Lord knew she'd be the first and likely – I was willing to bet my not insignificant savings balance – the last.

There was still one problem with that though.

Nico
What if she's too...peppy for me?

Bert
Bah humbug!
A little pep would do you good.

Nico
I'm not convinced.

Bert
Yeah, but you're a little slow on the uptake. You're allowed to like her.
Which is handy, because you do.

Nico
Say I did. I don't know how to be the kind of guy a girl wants long-term.

Her next text was a long time coming.

Bert
You just have to be yourself.

Nico
Yeah, I don't know how to do that without being a total dick.

Bert
Bahaha!

Sorry. No. Let me try again.
Not at all. You manage with
me all the time.

Nico
Yeah. I've never wanted
you.

Bert
Oh, wow. Rude. Thanks.

A second message came through just a tad too slow for my panicked heart.

No seriously, though. I'm
glad.

Thank fuck. I thought I'd almost lost my only confidant for a second.

Nico
You are?

Bert
Of course I am!
I love you, Nico. But we're
the friends type of
soulmates.

I didn't really know what that meant.

Nico
Thanks. I think.

Bert
No! that's a good thing. I
promise.

Nico
I'll take your word for it.

Bert
Do it slowly, then. Open up a little at a time, get her used to the idea of a different Nico.

I could do that. I presumed I could do that. The theory made sense.

By the time she's addicted to your body, she won't care you're more robot than human.

I felt myself frown, but I took no offence when Bert said things like that. She was allowed to. I knew she liked me as much for being more robot than human as she did my human qualities. I didn't have to be nice to her for her to think the world of me.

Nico
I suppose so.

Bert
In seriousness though, sometimes you just have to put yourself on the line.

Nico
You can say that.

Bert
You've gotta risk it for the biscuit, dude.

> **Nico**
> Except, in this case, the biscuit can reject me.

> **Bert**
> Yeah, not if you hold tight to those hang ups that stop you showing her your true self.

> **Nico**
> Hang ups?

> **Bert**
> Hang. Ups. You gotta just let those go and be yourself. Byeee!
> Take it from me, there are certain situations where you make allowances between what you *thought* you liked and what you actually like in real life.
> Let her see the real you and she'll come around. She can't not. It sounds like you're perfect for each other.

I wished. I knew she was perfect for me. I just wasn't sure I could be called perfect for anyone, no matter how much I wanted to be. I had some pretty deeply ingrained personality traits.

It wasn't a solid plan by any means. Raegan seemed really into the whole jarhead thing. Even if I could work out how to be a guy she was interested in, who could talk to her, and still be me, it was going to be a lot of hard work.

Something in me told me it was worth it, and I just hoped it would be.

17
Raegan

Something weird had happened to Nico. He was all of a sudden, out of nowhere, like this moody, sarcastic and yet awesome dude.

Later that afternoon, he just started talking to me again and I had no idea where that had come from. Except it wasn't just answers to me prattling the way I did best. He made comments out of the blue about things I was watching. Like when I was back on 'Doctor Who'.

"Whittaker was a good choice," he said randomly and I turned around to look at him.

I was aware my mouth was hanging open again and I snapped it shut. "What?"

He had his laptop open in front of him and was watching the telly over it. "After Capaldi, she was a good choice."

My eyes narrowed. "*You're* a Whovian?"

He shrugged. "I've watched it."

"You've…watched it. Okay…" I wasn't quite sure what to do with that information.

Suited jarheads weren't exactly the kind of guys I thought watched 'Doctor Who', let alone compared the different incarnations. He'd said his sister wasn't a nerd, but maybe he had a friend who was. Maybe it was an ex-girlfriend?

I excited myself by that idea. Excited myself and freaked myself out.

If he'd had a previously nerdy girlfriend, then my chances with him had just skyrocketed and that made for one very happy Raegan. If, on the other hand, he'd had a previously nerdy girlfriend, would that mean I had a lot to live up to? How did I compare? Was she…better at that stuff than me?

I thrust the panic out of my head. "You really like Whittaker?"

He nodded. "Compared to Capaldi anyway."

"Hmm."

"You disagree?"

"I do disagree. I don't like her at all." I held my hand

up before he argued; it was not a very popular opinion, but I stood by it. "I'll admit it took me a while to get used to the idea the doctor could change sex, and I'm willing to consider she's just been given *the* worst stories in the history of the show, but I don't like her. Capaldi at least did a god job."

Nico huffed a laugh. "He was terrible."

"No," I clarified. "Clara was terrible."

"Do you hate all women?" he teased.

"It kinda does sound that way, but no. I don't think." I paused. "No. I just think Clara ruined it. And don't get me started on the political bullshit they're currently shoving in our faces."

Nico inclined his head. "Yeah. All right, they've messed up this season."

I looked him over, too many questions to know where to start. Was he actually more my kind than I thought? Was he not totally wrong for me after all? Or, was it all mind games?

Later, I came up with a question to test him.

"Trek or Wars?" I asked, no context.

He looked at me like I needed my brain checked. "What?"

"Trek or Wars?"

"Pre-quel or Original?"

Oh, talk about me likey. Maybe he was a worthy adversary after all.

I walked over to him. "What do you think?"

"Original is always better."

"Borg. Better or worse?"

"Better."

That surprised me. "Why?"

"Darker."

"You like it dark?"

"Why do you ask?"

I leant on the table towards him and levelled a heady gaze at him. "I'm trying to work you out."

"Work me out?"

I nodded.

"I'm not disinterested, Raegan," he said.

I blinked. "What?"

His smirk was sinful and cocky and did those wibbly wobbly things to my insides. "It's not disinterest that made me say those things. It's my job to keep you safe. How can I, with confidence, say I'm doing my job if I let myself…get distracted?"

"You've got alarms to warn you if someone comes onto the block…"

I knew it was my life. I knew it was. But it was a little hard to take the whole thing seriously when the closest anyone had come to me was the office and that had been nearly a week earlier. Since then, as far as I knew, crickets. I felt totally safe with Nico. I felt like just having him in the house made any baddy think twice before he came after me. It wasn't lost on me that I was just that far gone for a guy totally wrong for me that I was willing to put my life on the line to be with him.

That was going to be conversation for future Raegan to have with herself about sorting her priorities lest she get killed – or worse, expelled…from life.

Nico licked his lips slowly like he was considering it. I wondered what in the hell I could do to help him along with that. Directness had worked in my favour before. I'd just be direct about what I was thinking, what I wanted.

"I don't know about you, but…I really enjoyed last night. Like, an unnecessary amount enjoyed. And would be quite partial to repeating. If you were up for it."

His eyebrow quirked. "Another dick joke?"

I shrugged cutely. "They're just there, begging to be

made."

"Begging?"

Oh, I liked that voice. That low, smooth, gravelly bedroom voice that went along with the heated bedroom eyes and made me feel like dissolving into a little puddle of wanton desire.

"Do you…like begging?" I asked him. Then I smiled. "No. You don't seem like the begging type."

"Is there something you wanted me to do, Raegan?" he asked me.

I leant closer towards him. "You want me to beg?"

His tongue ran across his teeth and Lord how I wished I was those teeth. "You only need to tell me once."

"You asked me yesterday if I liked it sweet or rough?"

He nodded slowly. "Yes?"

"I'll assume that was sweet by your standards."

Another slow nod. "Yes."

"Then I want you to show me what rough feels like."

He looked me over and his whole demeanour changed. I was instantly reminded of the predator.

"Bedroom. Now."

I stood up straight and nodded. "Okay then."

I hurried to the bedroom like a good little girl. I'd

barely turned to face him again when he came right up against me, crowding me with his body. Excitement fluttered through me.

"Take your fucking panties off," he said, his voice little more than a low growl.

I honestly wouldn't have said I was the type of girl who'd like that. But it was Nico. Of course I liked it.

I slipped my yoga pants off and my undies went right with them. Nico looked me over as his fingers played with the hem of my t-shirt. I felt inspected. It was a weirdly sexy feeling.

Suddenly, he pulled my body to his and kissed me.

Well. I'd asked him for rough. His kiss was deliciously rough. His tongue swept in to claim me as he spun us around and pressed my back against the wall.

He pulled away long enough to rip his shirt over his head, then he was kissing me again. His fingers trailed over my clit and I felt myself shudder with the early stirrings of pleasure.

Just as I thought his touch would get more earnest, he flipped me around to lean my front against the wall. His lips went to my neck as his hand slid between my legs again. He pressed himself into me and I could feel how hard he was for me.

His fingers worked me, building up the pressure sure and steady. It wasn't slow and teasing. He had a purpose and he was going right for it.

My hand gripped his arm and my orgasm was just about to break when he suddenly flipped me around again and picked me up to slam me against the wall with my legs around his waist.

He kissed me hard. He kissed me hot.

I could feel his dick rubbing against me.

Nico reached under me and I felt him undo his pants. He held me up with nothing but our bodies pressed together while he slid a condom on, and then he was thrusting into me strong and hard.

I gripped his back and my head fell back against the wall as his dick began to finish what his fingers had started.

There was no slow build up. There were not sweet kisses. Nico pounded me hard and fast from the beginning.

My orgasm hit me just as hard and just as fast after he'd got me so close before. It was all I could do to hold on to him while he brought me so close again and again, tipping me over the edge in a near constant onslaught of pleasant tingling rushing through my body.

Just when I thought any normal person couldn't possibly go on, I felt him tense. His thrusts slowed slightly and pressed deeper. His lips went to my neck and he held me tightly as he came.

We stayed that way for a few moments, while we fought for breath.

Slowly, he helped me find my feet and I just focussed on breathing while he dealt with the condom.

"That was rough?" I panted.

"Rough enough."

I looked at him in disbelief. "Rough enough?"

The smirk he gave me as he nodded damn near melted me all over again.

As it was, he had me in bed not ten minutes later.

18
Nico

Maybe Bert had been right. I'd let go of the filter a bit, I'd let a little bit of the underlying Nico out and…we'd still ended up in bed.

I was glad about this for numerous reasons. Firstly, getting down and dirty saved the socially awkward Nico from trying to be natural. Unfortunately, natural Nico had flipflopped between some kind of seductive nerd who knew what he was talking about, to the flippant, moody wanker who had no time for humanity. It served the purpose of letting her know the real me, but also felt more forced the more normal I tried to be.

I'd been floating in and out of consciousness since she'd fallen asleep. The guilty part of me felt the need to be awake and monitoring to make up for the time I'd been distracted. Again. It was a shame that wasn't how it worked.

So, I was just staring at the ceiling, elbow behind my head, letting myself drift aimlessly while I tried not too hard to think about what time was acceptable to leave her bed.

"What?" I heard her whisper and looked over to find her on the phone. "Duncan, calm down. What's happened?"

That had me on alert. All thoughts of falling back to sleep were gone. I was awake and ready for action. I sat up.

In the meagre light, I saw Raegan turn to me. "What? Okay. Okay." She was scrabbling out of bed, pulling her bathrobe on and hurried out even before I put one foot out of the bed.

It wasn't the first time she'd put my training to shame and I was only more enamoured with her for it.

I pulled on my boxers and hurried after her to find her in her study and staring at her computer screens. In the recesses of my mind, the nerd in me got hard just looking at her set up. More pressing and at the front of my mind was the fact that the Olafson International was currently under attack from an SQL injection.

"What's wrong?" I asked.

But Raegan wasn't listening. She was doing her job.

"I can block it from here, but the lag is going to bite us in the arse," she said as he fingers flew over the keyboard. "Where are you?" She paused. "And Jackson? Yeah. Okay." She looked at me. "We'll be in as soon as possible."

I shook my head. "You're not going in."

Her eyes stayed fixed on mine. "We'll be there in ten minutes."

She hung up and pushed by me and headed for the bedroom.

"You're not going into the office," I repeated. "Not after a physical breach."

She was pulling her clothes on. "I get you might not understand this, Nico, but I can only do so much remotely. The remote servers at Olafson International is beyond disgusting. The lag alone will put me behind enough to fail at keeping them out."

"And Duncan and Jackson are unable to do this without you?"

She paused only long enough to give me a look that told me what she thought of that. "They'll do what they can. But their best internally is maybe as good as my best from here. There was a reason Duncan hired me," she said unapologetically. "I might not do it often, but I'm good at what I do."

Given the immediacy of issues I had to deal with, I didn't stop to swoon over her total self-confidence as she stood up for herself, half dressed in the semi-dark in the middle of the night.

"I have to go in, Nico."

"And if it's a front for a physical attack? If they're trying to draw you out?"

She dropped her hands with her jacket in them. "Then you'll earn whatever paycheck you're getting out of this."

"You won't take no for an answer, will you?"

She shook her head as she pulled on her jacket. "You're done bossing me around. If you shied away from doing what you had to because you might get hurt, what would you do?"

I could only argue with her for so long before I risked her walking out of the house without me. "This princess rescues herself?"

She slid on her glasses. "And the whole damn castle,

too."

"Let me get dressed."

Used to dressing quickly and efficiently, I was ready by the time she'd picked up her keys and laptop.

"We do this and you have to do as I tell you," I told her as we walked out to my SUV. I continued before she could argue, "I'm serious, Raegan. Anyone could be waiting. Our intel is spotty at best. You do what I say, when I say it, and not a second later. Understand?"

I pulled the passenger door open for her and she looked at me before she climbed in. "Okay."

I nodded, resisting the urge to kiss her before I closed the door and went around to the driver's side. Something felt final about whatever we were about to walk into. There was more than just the need to keep her safe that sent my Spidey-senses into overdrive. I had this sense that an end was in sight. What end, I didn't know. I just had to hope it wasn't her life.

I pulled to a stop directly in front of the garage lift when we got to Olafson International. Even if it hadn't been the middle of the night on a weekend, I still would have given zero fucks about parking protocols. The sooner I got her into the lift, the better.

My eyes constantly scanning, I got her out of the car and successfully in to the lift. I hit the close door button.

"Call Duncan," I ordered.

She nodded. "Hey, we're here." She looked at me. "He says come up."

I felt uneasy about it. On one hand, no alarms had been tripped on my system and I'd set them up throughout the Olafson international security system – I had notifications set to go off for physical breaches and on certain files of Olafson's – but I'd not really expected them to try to hack the servers. It just didn't fit with sending a physical breach team.

My mind whirled with possibilities when Raegan and I walked out of the lift. The hall was dark, the only lights the ones in the IT office. I could see Duncan and Jackson at computers, looking more than a little flustered.

"What can I do?" Raegan asked, shucking her jacket and sliding gracefully into her chair.

"Take over from me. I feel like I'm just being counterproductive."

She nodded and logged in to her computer. I watched as her fingers flew over the keyboard. A piece of hair fell into her eyes but she didn't seem to notice as she concentrated on the screen in front of her.

Jackson would say something in broken sentences to her now and then, and she'd reply just as intelligibly. They worked well together, but I could see Jackson was slowing her down. He was good, but he wasn't good enough.

"Ah, frak!" Raegan grumbled. "It's a trap!"

"Calm down, Admiral Akbar," I muttered and shouldered the useless pillock out of the way and took his place at his computer.

My fingers were flying over the keyboard, my eyes firmly planted on the screen. It took me a couple of seconds to realise that I was the only one doing anything. My eyes darted up between strokes.

"I'm good," I said. "But help would be better."

Raegan opened and closed her mouth. "You... That was..."

I nodded. "Can this wait? Or do you enjoy your life being in danger?"

She blinked, nodded, then went back to her computer.

We worked in silence and I resisted the urge to look at her now and then. I didn't often get distracted when I was knee deep in my zone, but thoughts kept swirling.

What did she think? Did she care?

"This feels more like luck than skill," she said absently.

"I'm not surprised. Fucking clunky," I muttered.

And it was. The difficulty in staying ahead of them was in them not following the expected routes. They were all over the place. My eyes flicked over at the targeting program. It was hovering over central Europe.

"Whoever they are, they're doing this in house."

"That's what they were," Raegan said, her fingers not slowing.

"What?" Duncan asked.

"There were pings. Glitches. I thought it was a virus, but they've been at this all week. I recognise it."

I rolled my eyes. "They spent a week trying to break in and this is the best they could do? Amateurs."

"Well, you'd know." I heard the sarcasm and snark in Raegan's voice.

My eyes flicked up to her quickly and I saw she'd spared a second to look at me, too. "You want them finding you? I can sit this one out."

"Feel free. I don't need your help."

"Then you're lucky it's my job."

"I thought you were going to sit this one out?"

I growled, wishing I'd brought my glasses. Not that there was any time to put them on. "I wasn't actually going to sit it out, was I?"

"This princess–"

"I know!" I cried. "Saves herself! Just take the assist and get off your high horse."

"*My* high horse?"

"Should you two not be concentrating?" Duncan interrupted.

"I am concentrating!" we both snapped, then spared one glare at each other before going back to it.

But we didn't argue more. I just focussed on what I was doing and what she was doing. Our methods weaved together like some intricately choreographed dance to form one very respectable defensive team.

We worked until we were finding ourselves in a more offensive position and had them running defence. It wasn't long until we had their server in our sights.

"Can you…?" she started.

"On it," I answered.

"Worm?"

I nodded. "I can. You?"

"No. You."

I threw a worm into their server which should give us more information about who they were. I directed the intel to the Grace Grayson databanks. Just as the first streams of data were going through, Raegan slammed their systems with a DDOS attack, they were overloaded, and they'd be stuck looking at blank screens.

I sat back in the chair and rubbed my eyes. I hadn't had excitement like that in a while. I loved a good system overhaul, but an old-fashioned hack-off was something else entirely. I almost looked up to share a smile with Raegan, but the fact I'd just given away my undeniable nerd status slammed into me.

I pulled myself out of the chair and gave a curt nod to Jackson.

He blinked rapidly and shook his head. "Any time," he said in awe.

I strode off to a corner and pulled up Chaos' number.

"Yeah?" he answered.

"We had–"

"I've spoken to Olafson."

"He got up for this?"

"He's upstairs. He'll want to talk to you. Did you get

a location?"

I gave him the coordinates. "We got pretty local, followed them back. They should be there."

"How much intel did you get?"

"I won't know until it finishes coming in. I didn't get a good look at how big they were." I heard a ping from the computer and went back to it. "Huh. Of course."

"What?" Chaos asked.

"The office breach was hired."

"Any one we know?"

"The name's familiar. I've sent you the details."

Chaos paused a moment then said, "No allegiance. Easily dealt with."

"What about the Europe situation?"

"I've called in some reinforcements. We should know soon whether or not Miss Lane's life is still in danger."

Him and his ability to multi-task put me to shame.

I nodded. "Clanton's team?" I guessed.

"He's the best in the region. He said give him three hours to report back. Lucky they were so close."

It was lucky. Too lucky. Coincidences like that didn't come around too often in a lifetime.

19
Raegan

Everything was slowly falling into place. It wasn't necessarily the right place, but it was a place. And what was falling into place was me starting to realise that Nico had been a nerd all along. The signs were there. And I, apparent nerd queen, had shrugged them off.

He knew about servers and networks and routing traffic.

He knew about frakking toasters.

He knew about Han's pants.

He knew about RAM.

He knew about Borg.

He'd smirked every time he saw one of my nerdy outfits. Before, I'd thought it was like an 'oh, I don't get that reference but aren't you cute, dressing like a child'. I realised now it hadn't been at all. It had been an 'I get that reference and I find it funny' thing.

How in the hells hadn't I realised he was the exact thing I'd been looking for? A total beast in the sheets and a nerd on the streets. The absolutely perfect man. Could I have got luckier?

Then I realised, maybe some part of me had known all along? Like the part that kept telling me we had an undeniable connection and off-the-charts chemistry and a one in a million attraction? Maybe that part had known what the rest of my brain had refused to notice and that was the only way it had known how to tell me?

"So…" I said when he'd finished on the phone and we were alone. "We should probably talk?"

He looked up at me from the computer he was fiddling with. "About what?"

"You're…not exactly what you seem are you?" I heard the accusation in my voice. I hadn't meant it, but it came out anyway.

His eyes went back to the computer. "I'm who the job needs me to be."

I couldn't deny that hurt a bit. "So, the last ten days has been all just a job?"

"I am what a client wants me to be. Olafson wanted a

grunt. Today, he needed a different skill set. I used it." His voice was cold, almost robotic as he slammed the lid of the laptop down and looked at me.

"Oh," was all I could say as I looked him over.

His posture was rigid, making him fill his suit out with a self-assured arrogance that was just as sexy as it had been when I first met him. What wasn't so attractive was the hardened glint in his eye like I disgusted him.

I wanted to ask how could it have been just a job after what we'd shared. I wanted to say something about how it had meant more to me. But the words just wouldn't come. I saw the look in his eyes and I couldn't help returning something similar.

That girl who'd decided long ago to walk to the beat of her own drum had been swallowed by the girl who defended herself against rejection by rejecting first, hiding behind a mask of blasé indifference. It had never served me well as a defence mechanism, but I couldn't help it.

"Nico," Duncan called from his office, where he'd been filling Mr Olafson in with Jackson, as the person who'd found the intrusion in the first place.

"Excuse me," Nico said curtly, then walked away.

I felt like that was it. Book closed. Any possible future I'd entertained for Nico and myself over the course of the last week was…kaput. And all I could do was watch my perfect man walk away, leaving me totally wrecked in his wake.

I watched the men talk for a moment, breathing deeply to keep the tears locked away. I was a strong independent woman who didn't need a man's validation. I was the self-rescuing princess. No man was going to make me feel lesser than.

All pretty sentiments and ones I wanted to live up to. It was just going to take me a minute.

"Olafson wants us up there," he said as he walked back out of Duncan's office and weaved his way towards me.

I looked at Nico. "What?"

"Olafson. Wants to talk to us in his office."

"He's actually here?"

Nico nodded. "He's here."

Dumbstruck that Mr Olafson would deign to be present in the middle of the night on a Sunday, I followed Nico back into the lift.

I noticed the change instantly. While he still seemed

generally wary, there was no more shielding me with his body like it was second nature, there was no more brief touches every time I was about to enter a room before him, and there was no more tense potential radiating off him like he was ready to pounce at a moment's notice.

When we got up to Mr Olafson's floor, Nico led me straight through to his office without stopping.

"We're here," he said to my boss.

"Good morning, the both of you. I believe thanks are in order, Raegan."

I pulled my sleeves over my hands. "It wasn't just me."

"No. No. I understand. Team effort."

I pointed to Nico. "It was mainly Nico."

I noticed Mr Olafson look at Nico with interest. "Nico?"

I nodded. "If he hadn't built the worm, we wouldn't have been able to find them or delay their reboot."

"Well. Well done, Nico," Mr Olafson said. But there was a knowing look that passed between them. "The Grace Grayson team must be even more versatile than I realised to have a man proficient in IT *and* protection detail."

"We aim to please, sir," Nico said, his voice that monotone.

"And please you did, I hear."

I jumped and hoped that no one actually knew that I'd been so stupid as to sleep with Nico when it had clearly meant nothing. Not that I was against meaningless, it just kinda sucked when it was only meaningless on one side.

"Thank you, sir." Nico gave him a piece of paper. "This is the information for the authorities. Miss Lane and I managed to track them to that IP address. With more time, I could have tracked the physical location—"

I was sure he'd told Kit that he had a physical location…? Just what kind of funky spy software did he *have* on that laptop and how in the hell could I get my hands on it to play with it?

"—but it seemed more pertinent to prevent the breach."

Mr Olafson nodded to Nico. "And I thank you for that. There is definitely some…" Here he shot a look at me. "…sensitive information on our servers."

Nico didn't look surprised to discover that. "Rest assured, it's all safe, sir."

Why did it sound like he knew the exact kind of information Mr Olafson had on our servers and that it was some seriously shady shit? I tried not to wonder how long it would take me to find said shady shit because that's what had got me into this mess in the first place. And that had been an accident. I could only imagine the mess I'd find myself in after intentionally looking for trouble.

Oh, well, I thought to myself. *I'm sure they wouldn't assign Nico to me twice in a row.*

No. Certainly by just looking at Nico, I was pretty sure he no longer wanted anything to do with me if he could help it. I didn't know what I'd done or what I'd said to make him shut down like that. It was like the revelation of his nerd side had brought out some inner… I didn't want to say he was embarrassed by it and therefore pushing me away as a reminder of it, but that's definitely what it felt like.

That or he really just didn't like a nerdy girl.

My chest hurt. I wasn't going to be quite so cliched as to say that it felt as though something in there was cracking it two or shattering into a million little pieces. It was a deeper ache that made my eyes hot and prickly, and gave me a scratchy heated lump in my throat.

I hadn't let anyone dismissing or rejecting me affect me for nearly ten years, but one cold look from Nico and

I felt all those teenage feelings of inadequacy and self-consciousness I thought I'd never have to deal with again.

There was no way I'd ever change who I was for someone else, but I still entertained a momentary fantasy of what life could be like with him if I did.

"Now," Mr Olafson said and I realised I'd tuned out to a significant portion of their conversation. "You'll make sure Kit sends me the latest invoice, won't you?"

Because I needed the reminder that I was nothing but a paycheck to the sex god that was Nico Daniels.

Nico nodded.

"Good," Mr Olafson said with a pleasant smile. "I understand you'll see Raegan home and, all going well, we'll see a return of our IT department in tomorrow morning?"

Nico nodded again. "Awaiting confirmation, but that's the plan."

I knew it wasn't the time, but I wanted to know what else that meant. Was that it? Was Nico going to pack up and leave? Would I never see him again?

Being safe had never felt so shitty.

20
Nico

A week on the dot.

Well, that had been fun. While it lasted.

There was no hiding it now. Raegan knew everything. Well, she knew I wasn't the hardened ex-military guy I was supposed to be. And she hadn't looked at me quite the same way since.

After being partially responsible for protecting Olafson's precious information, the man hadn't been quite as snooty about the slip up as I'd expected.

"The Grace Grayson team must be even more versatile than I realised to have a man proficient in IT *and* protection detail," was all he said on the matter.

The fact it was said with barely contained sarcastic condescension wasn't lost on me. As a man *proficient* in sarcastic condescension, I recognised it in others just as easily as I dished it out.

I didn't much care about his reaction – the bill would be paid in full regardless of whether I lived up to expectations or not after the work was done – it was Raegan's reaction I'd been interested in. And that conversation had given me the confirmation that she was no longer interested now the nerd light had shone dazzlingly brightly. There wasn't a lot I could do about that. Had I the time to introduce him slowly like I'd planned, it might have been a different situation. As it was, I'd gambled and lost before I'd even properly decided to play.

We went back to her place after speaking to Olafson and making sure he notified the authorities of the perpetrators' IP, keeping the actual location that I had manage to secure between the Grace Grayson team. I wasn't strictly off the job yet, but I had a feeling that it was only a matter of time before we got the final intel that Raegan's life could go back to normal.

After she opened the door, the first thing I did was start packing up my suits. For a guy who never wore them, I was glad I'd had some use of them after Chaos insisted I get them. Not that Petra hadn't had a brilliant time fitting me and enjoying making me squirm with her brand of aggressive flirting.

"So, uh… Is that it?"

It was the first thing she'd said since we'd left Olafson's office.

I nodded. "Intel is due soon. We'll know what next steps need to be taken then."

Still, she hovered, like she wanted to say something else.

"Something else you want to say?" I asked her. My voice was sharp, it was cold.

I sounded like Commander Terrell, all bark and worse bite.

When she didn't speak immediately, I looked up. She shook her head quickly.

"No. No. That was it."

I gave her a single nod.

My phone rang a few minutes later. It was Chaos.

"Clanton's intel suggests they only just found her. Confirmed they hired a professional to breach Olafson International. Confirmed no allegiance. We've got people on that. Tip says they know nothing more than that their system breach came from Olafson International and

Clanton's put them out of business well enough that's all the intel they'll be getting."

I knew how Clanton had taken them out of business.

"Someone's just going to take their place," I told him.

"They're unlikely to care about breaches of their enemy's intel."

"It'll make them more careful."

"Maybe it should. By all account's Miss Lane's good, but she's not equipped for this sort of thing."

I knew where that was heading. "I'm going hunting."

It wasn't a question. It wasn't even a surprise. I had banks full of their data for a reason.

"Clanton's keen on clean up. He said just aim him and he'll deal with it."

I nodded to myself. "I'm going hunting," I repeated in resignation. "O Lord out."

I hung up the phone and got more zealously into packing.

"You... You're going away?" she asked almost too quietly for me to hear.

"My job here is done. Boss has given me a new assignment."

"Just like that?"

I nodded again. "Just like that."

"You're leaving?"

I planted my hands on the table and looked at her. "You don't need me anymore."

"I don't?"

It's not like she was arguing my point. She wasn't refuting anything. There was no suggestion that she had any interest in keeping me in her life. She just seemed surprised the whole thing was over so quickly. So was I, but I was more focussed on getting out of there than questioning my boss.

"Your life is safe. As promised, it took a week. I won't be in your way any longer than necessary."

"Fine. It'll be nice to have the place to myself again."

If that didn't drive the nail in, I don't know what would.

"On behalf of Grace Grayson Security, my sincere apologies for invading your space. We thank you for your business."

"Great!" she huffed. "Awesome. Thanks. No. Thank *you* for your service."

She spun on her heel and walked into her study, slamming the door shut behind her.

I jumped at the bang, cursing the day Chaos had asked me how my suit collection was coming along.

Once I was packed and everything was in the car, I paused at the study door.

This was it. This would be the last time I spoke to her or saw or touched her. And I'd be lucky if I did one of those things. Forcing an air of professionalism I didn't feel, I knocked on the door.

"I'm done. All the gear's been taken down, so you'll have your full privacy back."

I swallowed and tried to make myself say something more personal, but I didn't know what to say. There was no need for the suave Nico, and nerd Nico had no idea what to say.

I lay my hand on the door for a moment and waited to see if she'd say anything. I was just about to give up waiting and walk away when the door opened and I stepped back from it hurriedly.

"Good bye, then."

I nodded. "Bye."

"I'll walk you out."

I nodded again. After she awkwardly pointed to the front door like I might have forgotten where it was, we started walking. We said nothing. At her front door, I let her open it for me.

One more nod, then I walked as quickly as I could to my SUV and went straight to the Grace Grayson offices.

"Nice to have you back, Nico," Flo said with a smile and I wondered what in the hell she was doing there on a Sunday.

"Here's our resident nerd saviour!" Rollie cried happily and I gave him a terse nod as I lugged the equipment to my office. "I'll get it."

Rollie grabbed a bunch of stuff out of the lift I hadn't been able to carry on the first trip – it had taken me multiple trips to get it into the lift from the car – and followed me to my office.

"So, how was it?" he asked, totally oblivious to my mood.

"It was a job," I answered.

He sighed. "Everyone else always gets the good jobs."

"You still banging on about the rock chick gig?" Hawk asked, appearing from the other hall. "Hey, Nico. You didn't want to do us all a favour and go home to freshen up first?"

I didn't have to ignore his quip because Rollie

answered him instead.

"I am telling you, I'd be perfect for it," he said as he put my gear down on the floor of my office.

"Well, tough titties. Tank's already on detail."

"But I would be so much better! She's given him the slip like three times now."

"It was one time," Hawk said. He looked at me behind Rollie's back and mouthed 'no, it wasn't' like I gave a fuck.

As they argued, I manoeuvred them out my office door.

"What do you think?" Rollie asked me.

With one hand on my office door, I shrugged. "Don't care." And closed the door on them.

There was a shit tonne of files to sort through and they weren't going to sort themselves. I figured I may as well get started on them. After all, what better way to get over the woman of your dreams than to get lost in work.

21
Raegan

My life was back to normal. Or, it was supposed to be.

I'd been back at work all that week, but I felt like I'd been wading through the days, not really present at all. One minute, I'd been in my little secure bubble with Nico. The next, my house seemed awfully big and empty, and being outside it felt unnatural and scary.

"I'm surprised you didn't sleep with him," Janice said.

I blinked and pretended I'd been focussing on her computer. "What?"

"Nico. I'm surprised you didn't sleep with him."

I looked at her in disbelief. "Excuse you?"

She grinned and leant towards me like she was about to drop the year's biggest gossip bomb. "They're infamous for it. The Grace Grayson boys. It's the best kept secret that they give their clients anything they…desire."

There was a plummeting feeling in my stomach and I had the sudden urge to throw up the whopping nothing I'd put in there all day.

"What? You mean, like escorts?"

Janice looked around. I just didn't know if she was worried or hoping someone would hear her. "I hear they're *very* good at happy endings." She held up her hands. "That's all I'll say on the matter."

Seriously? Sex was part of the job? I didn't know why I was surprised. A bunch of super sexy spies. Of course, it was par for the course that they'd sleep with their clients. I'd been such a besotted idiot I hadn't even considered it. There I was, thinking they were just good at security.

I said nothing more as I finished up reconfiguring her emails – again – then headed back to the Dungeon. I'd found it cramped all week, so every chance I had, I went to the computer in question instead of deal with it from my desk. That seemed at odds with my newfound wariness of the world and I couldn't explain the urge. But since when were paranoias sensible?

That night, I went out with Filmore and Mel. I'd

forced myself to agree, knowing I had to re-join the world at some point. I trusted the Grace Grayson team and Mr Olafson when they told me my life was no longer in danger. I was still wondering if the whole thing hadn't been a tad overzealous on Mr Olafson's part and I could have just gone about my life same as usual.

Then you wouldn't have met Nico, a small part reminded myself.

Yeah, and you wouldn't have your heart smashed to bits right now either, another bit added.

I was distracted from my self-pitying wallow by Filmore bumping me. "Penny for your thoughts."

I shrugged and stirred my drink with my straw. "Nothing, just still got this system upgrade wandering through my head." Which wasn't a total lie. I'd suggested to Duncan that it was time for an upgrade and he'd agreed.

"I get that, but we haven't seen you in two weeks!"

Had it really only been two weeks since I'd met Nico? It felt like a lifetime, and that still hadn't been enough time with him. I'd found myself dialling the number for Grace Grayson too many times in the last week, then made myself stop because what would I say to him? He'd made his position clear. All I could do now was move on.

"Yeah," Mel said, slurring a little. "Boo work! Yay us!"

I couldn't help but smile. "I agree. Boo work. But, mostly done now."

"Good," Mel said. "More drinking. I've lapped you like five times now. And you're still on the first lap."

Her new thing was running, so everything got compared in laps. Or so Filmore told me. I'd been a little more silent on the chat than I had been while Nico was practically living in my house.

Not that more drinking was going to solve all my problems, but maybe more drinking would at least distract me from them enough for the time being. If I was really lucky, I'd get over my problems while I wasn't looking. It might not have been the healthiest coping mechanism, but I told myself that was a job for future Raegan and her priorities.

A couple of hours later, I was sufficiently tipsy to be bearing all to Filmore and Mel. There had been a lot of drunken 'oohs' and 'aahs' in all the appropriate places as I'd given them a pretty detailed synopsis of the previous two weeks. Mel had also walloped me when she'd heard

I'd been in danger, then cheered when the baddies got beaten. Overall, I think I was forgiven for keeping them in the dark. At least on the security thing.

Because Mel was fixated on the Nico thing.

"Why didn't you tell us?" she whined.

I shrugged as I took another big sip of my drink. "Because he was a suit."

"Yeah, but he wasn't," she reminded me.

"Yeah, but I thought he was," I reminded her.

Mel nodded. "True. But he's not!"

"So you love him," Filmore said with a nod.

"I'm not so shallow that I only love him because he turned out to be a nerd."

"Mm, beast in the sheets and nerd in the streets," Mel mused happily.

"That's not your type," Filmore said.

She shook her head. "No, but it's Queen Rage's, and tonight is all about her."

Filmore nodded. "Good point. Excellent point. So, we should go to his house now and tell him we love him!"

"Yes!" Mel cried, throwing her arms up and sloshing drink everywhere.

"No!" I told them. "I don't know where he lives."

"No!" Mel agreed.

"Work then?" Filmore asked.

"I don't think they work at night," I said, shaking my head.

"Sounds like he worked you at night," Mel said, waggling her eyebrows suggestively.

I frowned at her.

She shook her head. "No. Bad Mel. Too soon." It wasn't a question. She knew.

I gave her a nod. "Next millennium will be too soon."

"Oh, you like him that much?" she asked, putting her arm around me.

"I like him that much."

"Then," proclaimed Filmore. "I put it to you that we should go to Coles, get ALL the ice cream, go to mine and watch sappy movies that make us cry."

"It's after midnight," I said as I looked at my phone. Then I remembered. "It's after midnight. Your Coles is open!"

He nodded sagely. "My Coles is open."

"Ye-es," Mel said.

"Let's do it."

We drained our drinks and Filmore got to finding an

Uber.

As we wandered drunkenly around Coles, dancing to their amazing middle of the night Coles Radio tunes, I counted myself more than lucky to have found friends like them. Friends who would put off their plans to wallow over a relationship I'd never really even had.

There was no reprimand. There was no, even teasingly, blame put on me for sleeping with my security guard and expecting it could be something more. They were legitimately just thinking about break-up protocol and what I needed to get it all out of my system.

22
Nico

Life sucked.

I was back in my safe and comfortable t-shirts and sneakers. My eyes weren't being punished on a daily basis. But in all other respects, life sucked.

There were those romance books that went on about how two weeks can change everything. I hadn't realised that went for guys too. Although, in this case it had been ten days and my world had turned upside down and inside out.

I'd found my perfect woman and she wasn't interested in me after she knew the truth about me. I knew I only had myself to blame for thinking she might have been different, thinking she might not have had the same aversions to mating with her own kind as so many in the past had, that she – for once in my life – might have found the brash, socially awkward Nico as tempting as the basic idiot in the suit.

Something hit me and I looked up to find Rollie in the doorway to my office.

"Quit moping," he said.

"I'm not moping. I'm busy. I've got two weeks of work to catch up on. You want your paycheck this month, leave me the fuck be."

"Oh," he trilled in his falsetto. "Look at me, I'm Nico. I got my heart smooshed and now I'm even more grumpy than usual." He said in his normal voice, "Join the fucking club, nerd boy."

"Ryder, one would have to get his head out of his own arse in order to have any real emotions," I said scathingly.

The team jostled and teased and said all kinds of shit to each other. It was a given and none of it meant anything except we spent too much time together and knew each other too well. It also meant we knew when someone wasn't joking around anymore. And I was beyond the point of joking now, I was fully committed to this self-destruction thing and I was happy to take any one and every one down with me.

He frowned at me. "Harsh, dude. Not cool." He shook

his head. "Not cool." And walked away.

A little while later, "Knock, knock?" accompanied an actual knocking on my office door.

I looked up from where I was spread-eagled on my sofa. Mustering a vague approximation of a welcome smile I waved her in.

"They call in reinforcements?" I asked Bert as she sat down in my visitor's chair. Other than Rollie, she was the only other person to use it.

She leant her elbows on her knees and looked at me with sympathy. "Rollie's sulking. He said you were mean."

"What's new?" I scoffed.

"What's new is you being meaner than usual."

I frowned at her, but I didn't begrudge her being there.

"Wanna talk about it?"

I shook my head. "Not really."

"Are you sure?"

I sighed and leant my head back on a cushion. "Anyone else," I told her. "Anyone else and I wouldn't have given a single shit what she thought."

Bert reached out for my hand and I let her take it. "It's not all that bad."

"How is it not all that bad?" I asked her. I sounded bitter because I was. "It's all right for you, with your sickening forever love."

She chuckled. "It's not all bad because now you know what I've known all along."

I looked at her suspiciously before going back to staring at the ceiling. "Oh, and what's that, then?"

"That you've got feelings."

"More's the pity."

"Nico…"

She didn't continue until I was looking at her again.

"Do you think – maybe – you might have over reacted?"

It was probably a good thing that she'd made me look at her because there was an apology but also a 'shut up and think about it' glint in her eyes.

"I'll apologise to Rollie if he's seriously got his knickers in a knot over it."

"That's not what I meant and you know it."

"Like you can talk. You and Chaos are polar opposites."

"Nico, that's not fair."

"I never said anything about fair," I said, swinging

myself up to face her. "I'm talking fact and fact is that none of you want to mate with your own kind."

She took my hand again and squeezed it. "I'm not Raegan and she's not me. Neither you nor I can speak for her."

"And yet you're trying to."

She sighed, but she wasn't going to give up on me. "No. I'll speak plainly for you. I'm asking you whether you might have read her wrong."

"I'm not stupid, Amber."

She nodded. "I know. I know you're not. But sometimes we don't see what's right in front of us when we're caught up in our own emotions."

I deflated. "I didn't read her wrong."

She stood up and held her arms out for me. "Come here."

I let her help me up and let her give me a hug.

"Now," she said, with her face buried in my chest. "I think this apologising to Rollie idea isn't a bad one."

I sighed as I rested my cheek on her head. "Do I have to?"

She patted my back. "Yes."

"Fine."

I reluctantly let her go, and went to find Rollie. Unsurprisingly, I found him eating his feelings in the War Room.

"What do you want now?" he huffed.

I noticed Chaos, Hawk and Tank had followed me and were hovering in the doorway. Bert was nowhere to be seen; she knew when something was a team matter.

I cleared my throat. "I should apologise."

Rollie looked at me expectantly. "Well, go on then."

I frowned. "What?"

"That doesn't count."

"Why not?"

"That's not an apology, that's you saying you should apologise but not actually apologising."

I was starting to rethink my willingness to apologise to him. I'd much rather go and wallow in the dark alone and have the wanker angry with me.

"You want to come here and say that?" I asked, stepping forward.

Rollie's eyes narrowed as he stood up. "You want to go at it? I will wipe the floor with your sorry, miserable, moping arse."

"No one's going at it," Chaos said, his tone a warning.

"Leave the nerd be," Hawk said. "I haven't seen him touch a cup of coffee in days."

Rollie's shoulders dropped and he took a breath. "You get a pass this once, Nico."

I didn't want a pass.

"Good little Rollie, always doing what he's told."

I watched a muscle tick in his jaw. "You walk away, nerd."

"Come on, Nico. Take a breath," Chaos said.

I threw my hands in the air. "I don't want a breath. I don't want a pass. I don't want you tiptoeing around stupid Nico. I've not heard one nerd joke since I've been back. No quips about my coffee intake until now. And I'm yet to deal with any of Hawk's piss poor games of hide the tablet!"

"We get you're grieving, man," Hawk said. "We wanted to give you space."

"I don't need space. I'm not grieving!" I yelled.

"Sometimes we have to lose to see we loved," Tank said and I glared at him.

"And how would you know?" I spat, whirling to face him.

I was tall, but I still only came up to his shoulder. Tank

hadn't got his nickname for being virtually indestructible, though that had proved plausible on more than one occasion.

"You," I sneered, "over there in your ivory tower, looking down on the plebs who are dumb enough to fumble around in the dating pool and make idiots out of themselves! Like you'd know anything about it."

It was all bullshit, but I was looking for a fight. Not normally one for a physical showdown, just then I'd be more than happy if Tank wiped the floor with me and gave me at least a few minutes of distraction from thoughts of Raegan. He'd do a better job of it than Rollie. A more thorough job.

But, great wanker that he was, he didn't fall for it. "The people who love you will never leave you, Nico…" he said pointedly.

I looked at him blankly. What was he playing at? Raegan had showed no signs of loving me, but she'd certainly left me. Part of me wanted to think she was better off without me. It was a difficult thing to do when I knew I'd be better off with her. Which went a long way to prove she was definitely better off without my selfishness.

"The team, Nico," Tank said.

"What are you on about?"

"The team. We all love you. And I think it's high time we nutted up and told each other more often."

Curse him!

Curse him for knowing me better than I cared to know myself.

Curse him for seeing every little nuance of dynamic between the team.

Curse him for saying exactly the right thing whenever he deigned to open his mouth.

"Fine," I yelled. "I love you, guys." I threw my arms in the air and gave them a nod like that was that and what were they going to do about it.

Hawk nodded. "Same, guys. Love you, wankers."

Chaos smiled. "Love you, guys."

"I love you arseholes, too!" Rollie cried happily, arms spread like he was calling us all in for a hug.

"Nah, I'm good. Thanks," I told him.

"Get in here," Tank ordered and he and Rollie pulled everyone in for a group hug.

"Yeah. If this is going to become a thing, can we ask Rollie to shower first?" Hawk joked, fake gagging.

We let go of each other. Rollie and Hawk shoved each other companionably. Tank laughed. Chaos smiled. Even I spared them all a smile.

I might not have had Raegan, but I had my team and I knew they'd never leave me. It was more than a consolation prize, even if it wasn't that connection Chaos had talked about all that time ago.

23
Raegan

The lift doors opened and I saw a bright, clean foyer with a circular desk in the middle. It was the last place I wanted to be, but I was an adult and I could handle possibly running into Nico.

The woman at the desk looked up with a smile. "Welcome to Grace Grayson Security. Do you have an appointment?"

I bobbed my head as I walked forward. "Uh, Kit Grayson asked me to come in. Something about a debrief?"

She gave me a puzzled look.

"Oh, sorry. I'm Raegan Lane."

I saw the lightbulb go off. "Oh! Oh, yes. Of course. Yep. I know now. I'll just go and get him."

She jumped up and hurried down a corridor. I noticed

her look into a room to her right as she went, but she continued on and turned left. I rocked back and forth on my feet and looked around the space.

It was nice. The Grace Grayson offices. All big windows and polished floors. There were a couple of potted plants for greenery, but otherwise it was stark. Almost surgical. I wondered if it had anything to do with their military training or if the boys just liked the Spartan look.

"Thanks for coming in," I heard Kit say and I turned back to him with a smile.

"No worries. Least I could do after your team were willing to put their lives on the line for mine."

"Not at all. This way. Can I get you anything?"

I shook my head. "I'm fine, thanks."

"No? Coffee?"

I smiled, my eyes darting around in the hopes of getting a warning before bumping into Nico. "No. Thanks."

He led me into an office and indicated I sit down on a chair in front of a desk. He sat on the other side, facing the door.

"We just like to get clients in after a job, go through a

few things with them. Customer satisfaction."

I nodded but said nothing about what Janice had said. "Of course."

"Now, we've followed up with Mr Olafson and he confirms the authorities assured they have apprehended the responsible parties. He had no other details, but we have final confirmation that you're in the clear."

Which I thought we'd had weeks ago, but maybe that was the point of a debrief. I nodded. "Great. Good to hear. Thanks."

"Mr Olafson said he would let us know if there were any more problems."

Something about the way he was talking sounded stilted, unnatural even. Considering he was the boss, I highly doubted it was due to a lack of practice at this sort of thing.

"Ah, Nico," Kit said nonchalantly, looking at me.

Maybe he'd been worried about me running into Nico. No doubt the team had some idea what a fool I'd made of myself.

"Yeah?" Nico's voice was as familiar as coming home.

I couldn't help turning around to look at him.

He was paused outside Kit's door like he'd been caught walking by. His eyes dropped as he took a bite of a yellow iced doughnut, and I saw him swallow hard when he saw me. As he cleared his throat, he looked at Kit, but I was too busy drinking him in to properly register the look on his face at the time.

I'd missed him. I couldn't pretend I hadn't. But it wasn't just his touch I'd missed. Seeing him now, I knew I'd miss him far more after today.

He was perfection.

Sure, the tailored suits had been awesome. He'd looked mighty fine and I'd totally fallen for it. But this? This was what dreams were made of.

Converse.

Chinos.

Nerdy-arse t-shirt with a whole lotta fandom robots on it.

And, blow me down. Glasses.

I had never been more attracted to a guy than I was to that particular guy at that particular time. But I didn't know how he felt about me so I tried to reign it in.

"Nico, hi," I said, trying for a coy smile but feeling stiff.

He inclined his head. "Raegan."

Kit waved Nico in and Nico side stepped into the office awkwardly, like he'd rather be anywhere else on the planet.

"Everything okay?" he asked, his eyes now firmly on Kit as though they'd never leave.

Kit nodded. "Fine. I was just debriefing Miss Lane. You know. Protocol."

"Protocol?" Nico said slowly as a frown crossed his face.

"Oi, Chaos?" I heard another voice call.

"Yeah?" Kit called back.

"Can I borrow you for two seconds?"

Nico's frown grew. "I was just in there with him," he said as though that meant something.

Kit shrugged as he stood up. "You know Rollie, always with the worst timing. Excuse me a moment, Miss Lane, I'll be right back. Nico, hang around a second, will you? We should do a full debrief together."

Nico followed Kit as he walked out of the office. He opened his mouth, then shut it again. He looked at me, then after his boss, then at me again.

"Hi," he said.

I nodded. "Hi."

I desperately wanted to say something to him about how much I'd missed him. I wanted to tell him I missed our nights of not talking to each other and feeling like we were in each other's way. I wanted to tell him that I missed watching telly with him. I was almost obsessive enough that I wanted to tell him I missed my life being in potential danger if it meant he was with me.

I said none of those things, because he was fidgeting with his coffee cup and avoiding looking at me like I'd turn him to stone if he did.

It made no sense.

Had he been nothing more than the suited jarhead, I could easily believe that he had no interest in me beyond me throwing myself at him while we were in close quarters. I could see how he'd have had his fun while I was right in front of him and not cared any more about me when his job was done. But he wasn't just a suited jarhead. He was my kind. My people. My person.

It was hurtful and confusing that he'd just brushed me off since I'd learned the truth about him. Why was it not okay I was like him? What was wrong with me that he could just walk away? Maybe it wasn't me he was embarrassed by. Maybe it was him. Maybe he was embarrassed he was a nerd and so he hated all of us.

"Is it just me?" I heard myself ask then, realising I may as well get it out, I doubled-down. "Is it just me who's not good enough for you? Or are you not good enough for yourself?"

Nico looked at me and blinked. "Excuse me?"

"Is it just me, or does the nerd thing in general turn you off?"

"Turn me…off?"

I rolled my eyes. "Yes. I'm perfectly aware you have the ability to be turned on, so I know it's not a performance issue. Do you just prefer a higher class of partner?"

He spluttered. "A higher class of partner? I'm glad I made such an impression that you think just anyone would do."

"It's difficult to know what to think when you weren't exactly forthcoming with the truth about who you were, were you?" Why was I suddenly standing?

"I was doing a job," he said. "That job had certain requirements, which I fulfilled to the best of my ability."

I scoffed. "Oh, and you fulfilled them admirably. I'd

heard every Grace Grayson contract comes with a sex clause! I don't want to know what's wrong with you all, to have to charge for sex." I paused, realising what I'd said. "No. Wait—"

"None of our contracts come with a sex clause."

"It's just a coincidence then that you all sleep with your clients."

He pointed at me, mouth open to say something, then closed it and lowered his hand. "We don't all sleep with the clients. These day's it's just Rollie."

"And you."

"I slept with one client. If I ate roast beef once in my life, you'd hardly say I ate all the roast beef."

Even a bastardised 'Red Dwarf' quote – intentional or not – wasn't going to distract me from my annoyance.

"So, I was lucky number one then, good for me."

"You're not lucky anything," was his response.

"No? Oh, thanks."

He rolled his eyes. "I didn't mean… I meant… It was my first time in the field. The only time in the field."

"I was so bad that you're never going in the field again?"

"What? No. That's stupid. I'm the tech guy."

"Oh, are you?" I asked sarcastically. After the way he helped me deal with the breach, I believed he was the tech guy. I was just so annoyed with him.

"I don't even know why you're angry with me!"

"Because you left and didn't say anything."

"Me? I'm not the one who made it abundantly clear they preferred the suit over the nerd!" he said, voice raised in frustration.

My mouth dropped. Had my nan seen me, she'd have told me I was going to catch flies. I didn't care.

"You think…?"

He scoffed. "You're not the first one. It shouldn't've surprised me really. I know, out of the suit, I'm not exactly warm and cuddly. I'm brash and abrasive and not fit to be around actual humans. I get now that I was afraid to let someone see the real me. But was I wrong? First sign of the real me and you close off like–"

"You forgot arrogant," I told him stonily.

"I beg your pardon?"

"In your list of faults, you forgot arrogant." He opened his mouth to say something but I ploughed on. "I'm not the one who closed off, Nico. You were. I watched you coding and nearly fell in love with you on the spot. The way you stayed ahead of them, I…" I sighed appreciatively. "It was pure magic."

"You didn't…?" He cleared his throat and shifted his weight. "The nerd thing…?" He pointed to himself.

"Bigger turn on than the suit."

"And the suit…?"

I nodded. "Drove me crazy with lust."

He pressed his lips together and nodded once. He looked like he was going to turn around, then stopped and looked at me again. "You…" He gave a humourless laugh. "You like…?" He pointed at himself again.

"Big fan," I told him.

"Not just…?"

I shook my head. "Great and all, but I was actually wondering what in the hell I was doing obsessing over you when I thought you were nothing but a suited jarhead."

He smirked for a second. "Suited jarhead." Then focussed again. "So, you…?"

I nodded.

"And I…?"

"Uh huh."

"Huh. Well, fuck."

I was all for him seeming pleased that I'd actually preferred the nerd Nico, but it didn't exactly reciprocate my feelings.

"Is that a good 'well, fuck'?" I asked.

He rubbed his hand over his jaw and looked at me. "Uh. Yeah. Yes. Definitely."

I nodded slowly, hoping he was going to expand on that. When he didn't, I gave up hope that he reciprocated my feelings and realised he was just happy at being liked for him. Good for him, I guessed.

"Well, how nice for you. Do you know how long Kit will be? I really should get back to work."

Nico looked at me like I'd pulled him out of thought. "What? Um. No. I don't. Sorry."

"No worries. Just tell him I had to go. He can catch me up on email or phone or whatever."

Nico looked confused for a moment, then nodded. "Sure. I'll tell him."

I gave him a final nod, then made my way back out towards the foyer.

"Well?" I head Kit say behind me.

"What?" Nico asked.

"What, what?" came another voice.

"I dunno. What, what?" asked Nico.

"Fuck's sake, idiot!" someone hissed as I heard a, "Raegan!"

I took a breath and turned around, giving the receptionist a tense smile as I did. All I wanted was to get out of there and get started on getting over the humiliation that was telling a guy you basically fell in love with him and get crickets back.

Rollie jogged towards me. "Raegan," he said, a smile growing on his face as he came to a stop in front of me. "What the nerd meant to say was that he's madly in love with you and wants to have all your babies."

"Rollie!" Nico snapped and I saw Kit smirking.

I looked between them all and didn't really know what to say. This had a very high school, someone being set up for heartache and embarrassment feel about it.

"He's an idiot–" Rollie started.

"I'm not," Nico huffed.

Rollie kicked his head to the side. "He is. See, we joke Nico's a robot. Clearly he's not because he's obviously in love with you and I hear that's impossible for robots–"

"Rollie," I said gently. "I really should go."

Rollie shook his head. "No. You can't until you make up."

I licked my lip and took a deep breath. "No harm. No foul. All made up. It was nice–"

"He doesn't know how to talk to people," Rollie said. "Not really."

"Rollie, shut up," Nico told him and I saw Kit was holding him back. It was nothing more than a hand on his arm but it spoke volumes.

I felt like I knew what Rollie was trying to do. However, it only worked when both sides liked each other.

"Thanks, Rollie. I appreciate it, but it's okay."

"It's not okay," Rollie said earnestly. "You two love each other and are going to spend the rest of your lives miserable without each other because Nico's got the emotional range of a teaspoon."

We looked at each other and I felt like a lifetime of understanding passed between us. I could have been really good friends with the guy in another lifetime.

"It is okay, Rollie."

"It's just so sad."

I shrugged, patting his arm. "I'll get over it."

As I turned to leave, I heard Nico cry, "Wait. What?"

I stopped and gave him a sad smile. "I'm glad I met you, Nico." I looked to Rollie. "A true pleasure."

Rollie nodded, his eyes sad. "Same, Raegan. Same."

I gave everyone a smile and got into the waiting lift. I forced my face to stay neutral and I busied myself with my phone while the doors took a thousand years to close. Just before they closed, just before I was free, a hand slammed between them and the doors opened again.

Nico was standing there, a look of consternation on his gorgeous face.

"Wait. You mean you actually like me? Long-term?"

I blinked. "Are you actually that dense?" I asked.

"Look, I'm actually not surprised to find I am," he said.

It was still not a declaration on his part, despite Rollie's assertions, but what did I really lose by making him feel good about himself?

So, I nodded. "Yeah, Nico. I like you. Long-term."

"Long-term." He sounded like he didn't believe it."

I nodded again. "You can rescue this princess anytime."

He shook his head. "You're a queen."

I rolled my eyes. "Yeah. Of the nerds, maybe."

"And he's your king!" Rollie cried.

"Queen's consort, maybe," I teased Nico. "If he wants."

For the space of too many heartbeats, I thought that was it. I could easily picture him thanking me, pulling his hand off the door of the lift, letting the doors close and never seeing me again.

Time stretched on and it felt like the whole world was waiting with baited breath to see what he'd do in response. Which was crackers, because the rest of the world had far bigger problems than if the guy I liked liked me back.

Finally, he surged forward. His eyes were glued to mine like I was some kind of lifeline. His hand hit a button on the lift panel before, in one smooth movement, he closed the gap between us and pulled me to him while the lift doors closed on a whooping Rollie. One hand went to my neck as the other wrapped around my body, and his lips found mine. It was smooth and suave and perfect. It was like some move we'd choreographed and had to practice a thousand times before we got it right.

At least it was until our glasses crashed together.

I pulled away from him slightly with a laugh on my lips. "That's new."

He looked me over like my glasses offended him. "Yeah, we're going to have to do something about that."

"I heard practice makes perfect," I said.

He focussed on my eyes again and I saw a smile in his. "Yeah?"

I nodded. "Yeah. 'Kissing without banging glasses'. I'm sure that's a relationship cheevo."

He grinned. "I assume that comes after the 'girlfriend' cheevo?"

I swallowed a happy lump in my throat. "The 'girlfriend' cheevo?"

"What do you say? Will you unlock my 'girlfriend' cheevo?"

I didn't think I'd heard anything more sweet and nerdy and romantic in my life. I couldn't help but nod. "Okay. Yeah. Let's give this a whirl."

One eyebrow rose. "You're thinking about coffee?"

"Aren't you?" I teased.

He wrapped his other arm around me and his nose nuzzled into my neck. "Not this time."

Neither of us went back to work that day.

24
Nico

"Slow down," I heard Chaos saying. "Tank, slow down. Where did you lose her?"

I looked up because that, of course, helps one listen better.

"I've never known you to give up before."

That had my attention. I pulled myself up from my desk and strode to the boss' office and leant in the door. He looked up at me with a grimace and I waited to see what was happening.

"No. Well, I don't doubt you. Did you talk to their manager?" A pause. "She agreed?" Another pause. "What sort of different approach did you have in mind?" Pause. And a panicked look to me. "Seriously?" A pause and a nod. "Give me a bit to think about it. Just do your best for now. I'll talk to the manager and see what we can do." A sigh and a pause. "Sure. See you tomorrow." He hung up and looked like that one phone call had aged him ten years.

"He lost her again?" I asked.

Chaos nodded. "She's slipperier than the twins covered in bubble bath."

I gave a short snort. Flo's twins loved a bubble bath.

"What?" he asked, eyes darting to me again.

I shrugged and helped myself to the spare chair in front of his desk. "Nothing. Just trying to picture the special forces Chaos comparing anything to two toddlers."

He spared me an absent smile. "Special forces Chaos wouldn't have done a lot of things."

I nodded. "True. What's CEO Chaos about to do?"

He sighed deeply. "Tank's good."

It sounded so close to a question I nodded. "Better than a lot of us in a lot of ways."

Chaos nodded. "And yet Nora keeps giving him the slip."

"He thinks you should give up the contract?"

Chaos shook his head. "No. He wants to reassign it."

I baulked. "I am not dressing up in a monkey suit

again."

A wry smirk lit his face for a second. "No. Tank seems to think Rollie's up to the task." He looked me dead in the eye. "What do you think?"

I frowned. "Well, aside from his manic enthusiasm, I don't disagree."

"That's not a strong case for him."

I shrugged. "Rollie's exuberant. He'll be overexcited he's guarding a proper celebrity. But that doesn't mean he won't get the job done."

"You think he has the discipline?"

I smiled. "I think he has just the right lack of discipline that could make it work."

His eyebrows rose momentarily. "Tank said much the same."

"Then what are you asking me for?"

"I'm the CEO on paper, but let's not pretend this isn't a democracy."

"Yeah," I huffed a laugh. "It's a democracy when you don't want to take the blame for a wrong decision."

"I thought that's what a good boss does."

"Take all the credit but none of the blame?" I clarified.

"That."

It did him a slight disservice to imply he wouldn't take the blame. Chaos would take the blame from any of us, no matter whether he deserved it or not.

"So," he continued. "You think yes to Rollie getting the job?"

"He could hardly lead her further astray. If anything, she'll lead him astray."

"That had crossed my mind."

"Let him do it. He'll be ecstatic."

"Yes, but PR nightmare ecstatic, or contain the situation ecstatic?"

"Both?"

Chaos took a deep breath. "Both is…"

"Good?"

"Not bad. Better than the PR nightmare of a protection detail who keep on losing their client."

I spared him a split-second grin then hauled myself out of the chair. "Don't forget to lock up on your way out."

"You leaving before midnight?" He pretended to be shocked.

I nodded. "I promised Rae we'd finish the Lord of the Rings tonight."

"Theatre or Extended edition?" he asked so casually I forgot who I was talking to for a moment.

"Bert really did a number on you." But I smiled.

He grinned. "She did. Don't hate it. Not an answer."

"Extended."

"Good choice."

"In women or movies?"

"Both." He smiled.

I had nothing to say to that. He knew he was right. So, I just nodded, patted his door twice for good measure, then headed out.

****

"Oh my, God. Let me do it!" Raegan sighed with a loving smile.

I took my hands off my tie and looked at her. "I am quite capable of tying my own tie."

"Tell that to the mess at your neck," she chastised.

"It's not *my* wedding," I huffed.

I froze.

Did that imply I *never* wanted to marry? Did I want to imply that? Did she not notice, and I was worrying unnecessarily?

"Not…uh…" I cleared my throat.

She finished with my tie and looked at me in amusement. "Not, uh, what?"

I pulled a little on the newly tied tie. "Not that I'm against marriage."

Her eyebrow quirked up. There was a teasing lilt to her lips. "Really?"

I shook my head. "One day. Right woman. All that."

She nodded. "Good to know. I'm also…not against marriage. I'd definitely be up to marrying. Someone. The right someone. When the time came… Was right… You know?"

Her sentence started teasing and ended slightly flustered.

I felt hot in my stupid monkey suit. Not the good kind. I'd hoped the end of guarding her would be the end of monkey suits for longer. "Good. Awesome. So we… We feel the same about marriage? Theoretically."

"Yes. Theoretically. Not – like – literally because we… I mean, way too soon to even be thinking about marriage," she chuckled humourlessly.

"Totally. Too soon. Much."

"And, I mean, kids? WAY down the line. Like out of sight down the line." Her eyes widened like she hadn't meant to say it.

I hadn't thought seriously about kids. Not before now. Not before her. Or rather, I'd had no reason to think of them as anything other than alien entities completely devoid of boundaries or purpose. Flo's twins had a certain charm…provided I was nowhere near them.

With Raegan, I had this image of a couple of kids dressed up as Hawkeye, or Rey, or Pippin, and I didn't hate it. I liked it. I could deal with kids if they were half her.

I nodded. "Yes. Way later. But one day. Who else will agree with me that the Timeless Child storyline sucked?"

She bit her lip like she was trying not to smile too hard. "Well, I certainly won't."

I shook my head and wrapped her up in my arms. "No. You won't." I nudged her nose with mine. "I'm tempted to tell you that you have terrible taste."

"But you won't because you know I'll mention how my taste extends to you, and you're far too arrogant to allow such a thing."

She wasn't totally wrong. "Exactly." I nodded.

She laughed. "Well, then instead I'll say we should probably go. It won't look good if one of the groomsmen arrive after the bride."

I rolled my eyes. "Yeah. Fine."

She turned and grabbed her purse, but I caught her hand and pulled her back to my arms.

"I love you," I told her.

She smiled. "I know."

Grace Grayson Security

The Grace Grayson team all have their own story to tell.

Next up is Ryder. Read on for more info.

Rollie & the Rocker

See what all your favourite characters are up to down the track and maybe meet some new ones in Ryder's story.

NORA
As the female bassist in an otherwise all-male rockband, I had an image to maintain – relaxed, laidback, available; One-Night Nora. My freedom meant everything to me and that freedom had become my brand. Until I get a stalker and our manager hires a dude from Grace Grayson.

He's the sort of guy who can rock my whole world, if I could just roll with it. And he's making it harder and harder to pretend it means nothing. After all, rock and roll just go together.

RYDER
Eventually the boss man let me have the VIP. But some one-night rocker she turns out to be. The woman isn't falling for any of my numerous charms, no matter how close I seem to get. But the more time I spend with her, the more I don't mind. This is one good thing I never want to end.

She's the sort of woman to rock my whole world, if only she'd just roll with it. I'll have to pull out all the stops, but I'll do it to prove it to her. After all, rock and roll just go together.

[Buy now.](#)

O Lord & the Queen

Thank you so much for reading this story! Word of mouth is super valuable to authors. So, if you have a few moments to rate/review Raegan and Nico's story – or, even just pass it on to a friend – I would be really appreciative.

Have you looked for my books in store, or at your local or school library and can't find them? Just let your friendly staff member or librarian know that they can order copies directly from LightningSource/Ingram.

If you want to keep up to date with my new releases, rambles and writing progress, sign up to my newsletter at https://landing.mailerlite.com/webforms/landing/y1n6q2 .

Follow me:

Thanks

First thanks go out to the beta readers, especially Julie and Kaity for being so up with my updates and for such quick and detailed feedback. It was great brainstorming with you. Bringing Nico to life and doing him justice would have been a million times harder without you.

Where would I be without some technical help along the way? Thanks to Monkey and Birley for helping me sound like I had some idea of what I was talking about in regards to comp-u-ters but within the parameters of making a cool hacking scene.

And, of course, massive thanks to my husband. I know it's not been easy to have me back at my ridiculous writing schedule so soon after our son's birth. I honestly appreciate every book you put up with me writing and count myself immeasurably lucky I found you. You're the L-piece to my square.

My Books

I'm working on my adult list, but you can find out about what I have planned at my website, as well as have a look at my older YA books;
www.elizabethstevens.com.au/after-dark.

About the Author

Writer. Reader. Perpetual student. Nerd.

Born in New Zealand to a Brit and an Australian, I am a writer with a passion for all things storytelling. I love reading, writing, TV and movies, gaming, and spending time with family and friends. I am an avid fan of British comedy, superheroes, and SuperWhoLock. I have too many favourite books, but I fell in love with reading after Isobelle Carmody's *Obernewtyn*. I am obsessed with all things mythological – my current focus being old-style Irish faeries. I live in Adelaide (South Australia) with my long-suffering husband, delirious dog, mad cat, two chickens, and a lazy turtle.

Contact me:
Email: contact@elizabethstevens.com.au
Website: www.elizabethstevens.com.au
Twitter: www.twitter.com/writer_iz
Instagram: www.instagram.com/writeriz
Facebook: https://www.facebook.com/elizabethstevens88/

Lightning Source UK Ltd.
Milton Keynes UK
UKHW010923021121
393249UK00001B/275